DOCTOR, LAWYER, INDIAN CHIEF

A Story of a Family Reunited

The Adventures of the Angel Oleo
Book Two

Thank you!
Audrey Levy

DR. AUDREY J. LEVY

PACIFIC STYLE BOOKS

www.audreylevy.com
audrey@audreylevy.com

Pacific Style Books
P.O. Box 10358
Marina Del Rey, CA 90295

Pacific Style Books are available at special discounts for bulk
purchases, sales promotion, fund-raising, or educational
purposes. Special editions can be created to specifications.
For details, contact Special Sales Department, Pacific Style
Publishers, P.O. Box 10358, Marina Del Rey, CA 90295.

ISBN 978-1-686078-96-5

Printed in the United States of America

First Edition—September, 2019

Cover and interior design by Frame25 Production
Cover photos by Kamenetskiy Konstantin c/o Shutterstock.com
and Oliver Denker c/o Shutterstock.com

For Jimmy, my Father, and my Brothers

Preface

Dear Reader,

Picture Oleo as a beautiful barefoot angel with a great smile, curly auburn hair, sparkling brown eyes, and a delicious mouth. She wears a flowing white dress and reclines in a green meadow full of wildflowers. It is dawn, and she watches the wildflowers gently blow in the wind.

I dreamed of an angel—her name was Oleo. She only existed as long as someone believed in her. And then she existed for that one person. Sort of like Tinker Bell from Peter Pan, but in Oleo's case, it only took one person. Tinker Bell needed all of the children, and the more children that chanted her name and wished for her to stay alive, the more her light became stronger and brighter.

Oleo's entire essence was light, and she was an angel for lost souls. The lost souls could be on any continent, dead or alive, on this plane or that plane, anywhere that consciousness existed. Oleo was there to help lost souls find their way to the next step of their existence, whatever that next step might be.

For some, it was taking the next step to something as mundane as the supermarket. For others, it was the next step after they stopped breathing, when we go to the unknowable place that some call heaven, and some call hell, and some simply think it is the end, the last stop.

Oleo helped us get where we were going, no matter the destination. She was there when everyone else had gone. She was there when no one else could hear. She was there when there was no life raft, but one still had to take just one more step in his or her personal journey.

Oleo's entire existence was one long, big adventure. She traveled from one lost soul to the next, never stopping, always there wherever she needed to be. Oleo could be in more than one place at a time, so if you and I both need her at the same time, as well as a starving child in China, Oleo can be there for all of us. She has been there since the beginning of time, and will be there until there is no more time.

These are the adventures of Oleo . . .
Oleo, talk to me please.

You are one woman, every woman, one person, every person. Gender doesn't matter. Sexual preference doesn't matter. Age, race, country of origin—none of it matters. Not even what language you speak. I am here for everyone, and only when you want me to be here.

I am here in the darkest hours before dawn, when everything feels unreal. I am here when you don't know if you are dreaming or awake— when you don't know where you are heading or when you will get there. I am there when it's snowing, raining, or the sun shines its brightest. I am there in a rainbow and in a snowflake. I am beautiful and I can be ugly, but I am always in the eye of the beholder. If there is someone there to hold me, I exist.

And so I leave your interest in me up to you. I truly am an angel of attraction rather than promotion. If you want to find me, you will. Some won't ever care to look, but for the ones that do, I am here always and in all ways.

Sleep well now, my child. All is in the universe the way all is supposed to be, even when we don't understand why. I am here while you sleep, and I am here while you are awake. I am here when you think about me, and I am here when you forget about me. I am but a thought away. Focus on me and you'll hear me. I won't keep you alive, but I can make your choice to stay alive a little more bearable for the time that your consciousness exists. Sleep now, child. No guilt about resting your soul. Rest is okay.

Take care,

Audrey :)

Prologue

. . . Once upon a time, a Princess named Elizabeth was born with the proverbial silver spoon in her mouth. Her family hoped, that one day she would marry a rich and handsome prince, and they would all live happily ever after.

. . . But, instead . . . her brother Samuel became one of the biggest Hollywood power brokers in history, and Elizabeth got shot in the head by her nephew at her niece's wedding, and found herself halfway to heaven with an angel named Oleo, who just might be able to help the Princess change her destination.

1

"Holding on to anger is like grasping a hot coal with the intent of throwing it at someone else; you are the one who gets burned."
—Buddha

Elizabeth Elias, a slender woman with a tiny frame and dark hair askew on her pillow, had just gotten into bed when she heard a gunshot that would change her life forever . . .

≈

The piercing siren of an ambulance screamed through empty, silent streets of the hottest Christmas season in Los Angeles history. Inside, Elizabeth was stretched out on a gurney with the bullet she had heard lodged in her brain. Her blood seeped onto a white sheet. Elizabeth seemed so very fragile, while tubes and needles were being stuck into her.

Elizabeth's mind filled with vague images of people milling around her. She felt an incredibly intense pain in her head.

Everything was fuzzy. Elizabeth wondered if she was dreaming.

Gradually, a transparent Elizabeth gently floated out of her body, and hovered a few feet above at the ceiling of the ambulance. She saw a woman lying on the gurney, being worked on by two paramedics.

Elizabeth wrinkled her nose at the stink of death, and suddenly became aware that the woman on the gurney was herself. Elizabeth yelled in alarm, "Hey, that's me! What the hell is going on?"

The paramedics didn't react to Elizabeth's voice. One of the technicians shook his head in frustration, while his hands moved fast trying to save the unconscious woman. "Shit. . . Look at all this blood! There must be a bullet in her brain. I think this one's gonna be DOA."

DR. AUDREY J. LEVY

The other paramedic took a moment to wipe the sweat from his brow and said, "So much for a quiet Sunday."

Elizabeth could hear the ambulance techs talking about her, and impatiently tried again to get their attention. "Will you guys just wait a minute! I remember I was at a wedding. Everything seemed fine. Afterwards, I got into bed, and a gunshot rang out."

When the technicians didn't respond, Elizabeth yelled in frustration, "I have to get them to hear me!"

2

While the frantic paramedics did as much as their training would allow, Elizabeth suddenly found herself in a forest as a beautiful, unblemished woman. No longer part of her injured body in the ambulance, she was surrounded by the unbelievable sight of giant pine trees located in a valley between red majestic mountains. Elizabeth breathed deeply, taking in the powerful scent. She reached out to touch the incredibly detailed bark of one of the trees.

As Elizabeth studied it, the bark moved ever so slightly. In awe, Elizabeth whispered, "I can see the tree *breathing*." Her eyes opened wide in wonderment, as she took in her surroundings. "Where the hell am I?"

From the safety of the towering pine trees, Elizabeth watched as a stunningly groomed bald eagle soared through a striking blue sky, the white head blending with puffy white clouds. The eagle effortlessly scaled the mountains, and landed on one of the tall trees.

Elizabeth realized the eagle had spied her, and was now staring at her. She carefully sat down in the forest behind a huge tree trunk to get out of sight. Elizabeth didn't notice a mountain lion was hiding behind another tree, stalking her for his next meal . . . but the eagle saw it.

The bird watched as the mountain lion carefully crept into the clearing. The king of the jungle's sinewy muscles bulged with each cautious step. In an instant, the lion swept toward the unsuspecting Elizabeth, but the eagle was too fast . . .

It whooshed into the clearing between the lion and the woman, instantly transforming into an eight foot growling bear, that scared the hell out of the lion.

The bear lunged at the lion, swiping away, and the lion, not wanting any part of a losing fight, bounded off in the opposite direction. Terrified, Elizabeth said, "It'd be easier to get

Road Runner for breakfast, than mess with that bear!"

Elizabeth jumped up from her hiding place, preparing to make her break for freedom. The bear lowered her front paws to the ground, studying Elizabeth, and suddenly transformed into a beautiful woman with curly auburn hair, sparkling brown eyes, a delicious mouth, and a great smile.

The woman wore a flowing white dress and was barefoot. She tilted her head to one side, thinking, and abruptly a pair of sandals appeared in her right hand. She laughed out loud as she slipped on her shoes.

"Hi there. I'm Oleo."

Elizabeth's mouth quivered. "Noelle, thank God, it's you! I was so scared."

Oleo smiled. "I'm not Noelle. I'm Oleo, and you're okay now."

Elizabeth laughed. "Noelle Splendor, you can call yourself anything you want, but you just saved my life! You changed from an eagle into a bear, and saved my life!"

Oleo glanced over her shoulder. "I wouldn't mention that to too many people, if I were you. They might think you were a little, you know . . ." Oleo twirled her index finger next to her forehead to indicate 'crazy,' but Elizabeth couldn't contain her excitement.

"You whipped down off the top of that tree, changed into a bear, and scared the shit out of that lion!"

Oleo was nonplused. "Everything is possible here, Elizabeth."

"Why are you calling me Elizabeth? You always call me Lizzie." Now Elizabeth was really puzzled. "Noelle, what's going on?"

"Ms. Elias, listen to me. I'm not Noelle, but I do know everything about you."

Elizabeth's eyes indicated her fear. "Are you an angel? Am I dead?"

Oleo laughed. "Yes and no. Guess again."

Elizabeth tried to clear her head by rubbing her forehead. "The last thing I remember is being in an ambulance with a horrendous headache. I wondered if I was dying . . . Is this heaven?"

Oleo put a gentle hand on Elizabeth's shoulder. "No, dear. You've jumped ship into a near death experience, and we're only halfway to heaven. So, you could consider it sort of a parallel universe."

Elizabeth furrowed her brow, and cautiously backed away. "Ah, of course . . . why didn't I think of that?"

Oleo laughed. "Come. I'll show you your ambulance."

Oleo headed off through the forest. Elizabeth got her bearings, and with no other clues to follow, she hurried to catch up.

≈

3

Oleo broke through the trees with Elizabeth right behind her. "Hey! Wait a minute! What was your name again? Oliver?"

Oleo stopped abruptly, and Elizabeth bumped into her. "It's Oleo. I named myself that because I like to be able to slip in and out easily."

"Oleo? As in oleomargarine?"

"The very same."

Elizabeth wrinkled her nose. "Sounds greasy."

"I prefer to think of it as lubricious."

"Mmm. Sounds sexy."

"Take it anyway you wish. I'm glad to hear you verbalizing your healthy attitude toward sex."

Elizabeth blushed. "What makes you think it's so healthy?"

"I know everything about you . . . remember?"

Oleo started walking again. Elizabeth quickened her step. "What do you mean, 'yes and no'? And I thought there was only one universe. The whole meaning of the root word 'uni' is having or consisting of only 'one.'"

Oleo waved her hand dismissively. "Universe is a *human* word."

Elizabeth persisted. "But 'universe' means the totality of all things that exist!"

Oleo stopped in her tracks. She looked at Elizabeth with all of the loving in her eyes that one heart can have for another. "Humans created language to communicate about things they didn't understand and couldn't comprehend. Remember Columbus had to fight the concept that the world was flat. Galileo spent his life under house arrest, because he bucked the Catholic Church when he supported Copernicus's view that the sun didn't revolve around the earth."

Elizabeth shook her head emphatically. "I buy that the earth isn't the center of the universe, but the idea that there's *more* than one universe? I don't think so."

Oleo pondered for a moment. "I can see this is going to take longer than I thought . . . I think you'd better sit down."

"But I don't want to sit down! I'm in a hurry. I'm dying, remember? Didn't you hear that guy? He thinks I'm gonna be DOA. You know what that means, don't you?"

"Of course I do! Who do you think I am? Oh, I guess, you're not sure yet. All right, let's get some ground rules straight. DOA means Dead on Arrival. I know everything you know, except . . . well, what I know and what you *don't* know is going to take more than just a couple of minutes . . . so you're going to *have* to sit down."

Elizabeth plopped down on the ground, sitting cross-legged like an Indian. "There! How's that?"

Oleo smiled. "Good. Now, first we need something to keep you occupied long enough for me to really explain things to you. I think a nice meal is in order."

"What?!" Elizabeth was very confused.

Suddenly, they were in an idyllic garden with gushing waterfalls and rainbows all around them. They sat on a red checkered blanket with a complete picnic lunch and playful squirrels to boot. Elizabeth was astounded. "Wow! I can smell the flowers from here!"

Oleo seemed very satisfied. "What do you think? This is my place."

Elizabeth laughed in delight. All around her was the brightest and biggest green foliage she had ever seen. The clearest of clear water ran in a brook beside her, and birds filled the air with their sweet songs. "I can't remember why I was upset. . . oh yes, the ambulance. . ."

"Let me show you something." Oleo snapped her fingers and a big screen television appeared on their picnic blanket. Elizabeth did a double take at Oleo's magic, and Oleo turned on the TV. On the screen was the scene of the speeding ambulance.

"In your world, you're in that ambulance. In my world, you're here with me. In your world, I look like your best friend, Noelle Splendor. In my world, I'm called Oleo."

"But what do you mean when you say *your* world?"

"Remember reading 'Superman' comics when you were a kid?"

"Sure."

"Remember there were parallel universes and the Phantom Zone?"

"Yes."

Oleo took a deep breath and smiled proudly. "Welcome to my universe . . . Today, I'm an angel in the Fun Zone."

Elizabeth didn't understand. "But how did I get here?"

"It's your lucky day."

Elizabeth laughed. "Right! I'm on my way to being DOA."

"Yes, but the lucky part is that I'm in the middle of a treasure hunt in my universe, and one of the items I have to get is a forgotten person. I got the idea from one of your universe's old movies, 'My Man Godfrey.'"

"What are you talking about?"

"You, Elizabeth Elias, are a forgotten person."

Elizabeth stood up angrily. "Thanks a lot!"

"Well, you don't have to be angry with me! You're the one who has forgotten yourself."

"What's that supposed to mean?"

"Let's change the channel, and look at who you were a week ago today."

Oleo reached forward to change the channel. Elizabeth quickly pushed Oleo's hand away and turned off the TV. "I don't want to see that!"

"Why not?"

"I wasn't a pretty sight a week ago."

"All right, we'll watch an episode that happened a little earlier in your life . . . so you'll understand that your family loves you."

"I don't have a family!"

Oleo jumped up and squarely faced Elizabeth. "Will you give up your anger for just one minute, and watch?!"

Elizabeth narrowed her eyes at Oleo, and then her mood softened. "All right. . . but only because you look like my best friend, Noelle."

Oleo smiled. "Good. Now, please sit!"

≈

4

They both sat, and Oleo turned on the television. She switched the channel and they saw a black limousine pull away from a cemetery.

Inside the limousine was a three year old Elizabeth with her parents and her nine year old brother, Samuel. Everybody looked very sad except Elizabeth. With the innocence of childhood, she asked, "Why is everybody so sad?"

"Cuz Grandma's dead, stupid!"

Elizabeth's father, Elliot, intervened. "Sammy, don't call your sister stupid!"

"What's dead mean, Daddy?"

Elizabeth's parents exchanged a glance of 'how do we answer that one?' but Sammy blurted out his explanation. "It means, Lizzie, that we don't get to see Grandma anymore!

And we don't get to eat anymore of her chocolate chip cookies either!!"

Elizabeth started to cry. "Mommy, make Sammy stop it. It can't be true. He's lying!"

But Elizabeth's mother, Julie, cried also, too distraught with her own sorrow to counter her son's simple truth.

Sammy was triumphant. "See! I am *not* lying!! It's true. Mommy's mother is dead and she's *never* coming back!!"

Sammy angrily kicked the inside of the limo's door, the leather seats in front of him, and the carpeted floor. His parents tried to console him, and Elizabeth crawled into a corner to avoid her brother's flailing legs.

"Mommy, say it's not true! Daddy, say it!"

Elizabeth's father took her in his arms, and wiped away her tears with his fingers. "It is true, honey. Grandma died. One day everybody dies, so we need to be ready and prepared for that day."

Oleo shut off the television. Elizabeth tried not to show she'd been crying. "The only things I remember about my grandmother are that she smelled really good, she hugged me a lot, and

Sammy seemed to love her more than anyone else in the family. They were really close."

Oleo reassured her. "Your grandmother was a good woman."

"Well, the rest of my family didn't turn out to be very good."

"I know your parents left all their money to your brother, but that's no reason to hold a grudge against them forever."

"I stopped being angry with my parents a long time ago. They just never stopped seeing me as the baby, and figured Sammy would take care of me. But Samuel, who wanted to be the Indian Chief when we were kids playing Cowboys and Indians, and always cheated at Monopoly, had his own agenda for the money. He built one of the biggest talent agencies in Hollywood, Artists Creative Management, otherwise known as ACM. Samuel couldn't give two fucks about his sister, so I'm still at war with my brother."

Oleo spoke gently. "Put aside your war long enough to think about life from a different perspective."

"What perspective is that?"

"Someone with a bullet in her brain!"

"Who shot me anyway?"

"If I tell you who actually did it now, you won't change your future, you won't stay around till the end of the story, and I'll lose my treasure hunt."

Elizabeth suddenly saw the light. "Wait a minute, you mean, I can alter my future? As in, not getting shot?!"

Oleo nodded. "Yes, but it will take a lot of work on your part."

"Like what?"

"Like letting go of your anger, for one thing."

"I have a right to be angry! I've had a lot of shitty things happen to me, and besides, it keeps me safe from getting too close to those vultures called 'humans!' Don't tell me this is one of those touchy-feely games!"

Oleo resumed her formal attitude. "Ms. Elias, you don't seem to realize that your life has truly been interrupted, and there are things you really, REALLY need to do."

"I don't believe you! I think this is a dream!!"

"Are you willing to take that chance? Is letting go of your anger really that threatening?"

Elizabeth screwed up her face in frustration. "When I do the work, will this story have a happy ending?"

"I'm glad to hear you say 'when' instead of 'if,' Elizabeth. That indicates a positive attitude," answered Oleo.

"Well, I *know* the difference . . . duh!!!"

"Yes, of course, you do, but we shall see what actually happens, because as you also know, actions speak louder than words."

"Okay, so *when* I do the work, do I get a happy ending?"

"Of course. You want to sail away into the sunset, don't you?"

"Doesn't everybody?"

Oleo shook her head no, and with very serious eyes said, "You would be surprised at the amount of people, who have the opportunity, and don't take it . . . Are you ready to go back to last Sunday?"

Elizabeth shrugged her shoulders. She wasn't really sure. "I could sure use a drink first."

Oleo snapped her fingers. A silver tray appeared with an open bottle of champagne in an ice bucket and two filled glasses. Oleo gave one glass to Elizabeth and took the other. Oleo toasted. "To the French, my dear. An' zoh, mon cheri, leesten to this story. You are walking along the boulevard with your beautiful German Shepherd. A man dressed in surgeon's clothes says to you, 'What a beautiful dog.' You say, 'Oh, thank you, sir.' He says, 'Come with me to Tahiti, my love, and bring your K-Y jelly. . .'"

Surprised at the punchline, Elizabeth choked on her champagne. Oleo laughed. "With a little lubrication, we will watch, and you will find out how you might change your future."

Oleo turned on the TV.

~

5

It was just before dawn and a *Los Angeles Times* delivery truck, decked out for Christmas, worked its way up the curving street of Beverly Glen Blvd. The neighborhood nestled between Beverly Hills and Bel Air Estates was elaborately decorated for the holiday season.

A jeep with a Christmas wreath on its front hood followed the delivery truck. The driver threw out a Sunday *Times*, and it landed in a driveway next to a bunch of other newspapers, yellowed from the sun.

The jeep pulled into the driveway next door. Noelle Splendor, the human twin of Oleo, hopped out of the jeep, and ran up to the driver, who slowed to a stop. "Hi, Roger, how ya doin'?"

Roger handed Noelle a Sunday *Times*. "Okay, Noelle. Merry Christmas!"

"Hell, that was yesterday. Today's Boxing Day! Feel like a fight?"

Noelle performed a fancy karate kick. Roger laughed and feigned fear. "You oughta give one of those kicks to your weirdo neighbor, Elizabeth Elias. Have you met her yet?"

Noelle looked over her shoulder at the house next door with the yellowed newspapers piled up. She shook her head.

"Nope. Sometimes in the middle of the night I hear her vacuuming, but the shades are always drawn. Even Silvi's curious about her. She always goes straight over to the woman's door, when we go for our walk."

"Well, she must pay her *LA Times* bill," Roger said, "because I've been deliverin' papers here goin' on five years now. Every once in a while, I come by here, and all the papers are cleared away, but I never see any workmen."

"Yeah, I know," Noelle mused. "The hillside up behind her house is all overgrown too."

"Once a year, she has to have that hill cleared of the brush, or the Fire Department will get on her," Roger said.

Noelle nodded. "So I heard from my land-lord. You know, Roger, I've lived here since Labor Day, and I've met everybody in the neighborhood except my next door neighbor. What gives with that lady?"

Roger shrugged. "I don't know. You should go knock on her door."

Noelle shook her head. "Nah. I don't want to do that. Privacy is important to people."

"Just tell her, that you're her new neigh-bor, it's the Christmas season, and you thought you'd say hello."

"Right," Noelle laughed. "Maybe I should ask to borrow a cup of sugar . . . after all, it's only dawn!"

"Well, at least, at dawn," Roger said, "You can be sure she'll be home."

Noelle agreed. "Yes, I guess I haven't seen her sneaking in or out for any middle of the night trysts. Do you know anything else about her, Roger?"

"The guy up at the corner market says she's lived here as long as he can remember, and he's owned that store for about 15 years. A long time ago, she started ordering what she wants over the phone, and his kid delivers it to her."

"Hmm, maybe she's an agoraphobic."

"What's that?" Roger asked.

"One of those people who are afraid to go outside. They never go out."

"*Never?*"

"Nope. Never," Noelle said.

"That's crazy," Roger lifted his eyebrows and shook his head.

"Everybody's a little crazy, Roger. You know that."

"It's just cuz you work with those kind of people, Noelle, that you're so tolerant of everybody."

"My father used to say my mother and I would invite Hitler into tea . . ."

"Workin' the night shift and all . . . you must have some stories to tell about what goes on in that hospital psycho ward . . ."

Noelle shrugged her shoulders and saluted Roger. "I'm just a workin' girl, Roger. Happy New Year to you. I've gotta go walk Silvi."

Roger saluted back. "Same to you, Noelle. Have a good one."

Roger waved as he pulled away. Noelle walked up to her front door, and opened it to let out Silvi, a beautiful black and tan German

Shepherd with a very shiny coat, and a full bushy tail almost down to the ground. They greeted each other with lots of hugs, kisses, and murmuring.

"Hello, Silvi girl . . . How are you? Ready to play?"

Silvi yipped with joy and ran outside, as Noelle threw her keys and purse inside onto a small entryway table. She dropped the Sunday *Times* onto a chair, and closed the door behind her to join the Shepherd.

≈

6

Silvi immediately headed for the house next door that belonged to Elizabeth. She peed in the dirt in front of it. Noelle walked up to the main door. She rang the bell. When no one answered, she lightly knocked on the door. Still no response.

Noelle walked over to a window with Silvi close at her heels. Knocking on the window, Noelle called out, "Hello? Is anyone home? Hello???"

Still nothing. "Hmm, that's odd, Silvi. For a woman that never goes out, you'd think she'd answer her door, or at least, tell us to go away. Maybe she's scared of us. What do you think, girl?"

Noelle tried to peer inside. Silvi stood on her hind legs, and put her nose up to the glass. She used her paw to scratch at the dirt that had collected, but neither of them could see through the drawn blinds.

Noelle and Silvi walked around the house. Noelle found another window, which was slightly open, and she yelled through it. "Helloooooo? Anybody home?"

Nothing. Silvi sniffed the air that came through the crack. Noelle peeked through the open window. She saw Elizabeth's slender frame sprawled on the couch with her head underneath a pillow. She wore faded jeans and a T-shirt with food stains on it. Her arm hung down to the floor next to a knocked over empty bottle of wine, a baggie of pot, and a pipe. An empty bottle of pills was on its side next to them.

"Uh oh, Silvi, we got trouble here." Noelle paced, thinking, and Silvi tried to push the window further open with her nose. "All right, girl. Let's do it."

Noelle squeezed her arm through the small opening of the window. She felt around until her hand found the handle. Noelle rotated it to open the window wider. Now she could see inside, and what she saw was a living room in shambles. Flies feasted on spoiled food. Books and newspapers littered the floor.

Noelle managed to make an opening wide enough for herself to crawl through. Silvi jumped in right behind her. They walked over to Elizabeth, stepping over bent aluminum cans of soda, magazines and newspapers, both of them sniffing the air. "Whew, it stinks in here, Silvi."

Noelle cautiously approached Elizabeth. "Hello . . . lady . . . are you awake?"

Elizabeth didn't move. Silvi explored the woman with her nose, and Noelle carefully took the pillow off of Elizabeth's head, gently feeling her tiny wrist.

"We've got a pulse, Silvi, so we don't need to call 911 just yet."

Noelle gently turned Elizabeth over. She was thin and drawn. Not much color in her face. Noelle touched Elizabeth's skin with the back of her own hand.

"Cold and clammy. Not good. C'mon, Silvi."

As Noelle lifted Elizabeth off the couch, and carried her to the bathroom, Elizabeth started to stir.

"Who are you?" she murmured.

"Your neighbor," Noelle answered, as she placed Elizabeth into the bathtub and turned on the shower head. Elizabeth immediately came to complete consciousness, and tried to pull herself out of the way of the water.

"HEY!!! What do you think you're doing?!"

But Noelle was stronger, and in better shape, so she just held Elizabeth under the stream. "Waking you up."

"Bitchen! Let me outta here! I'm getting all wet!!"

Elizabeth struggled to get away from the shower, but Noelle restrained her. In the process, they both got soaked, and Silvi started to bark with excitement.

"A dog!" Elizabeth exclaimed. "Where'd a dog come from?"

"Just stay in the shower for a minute. Sober up a bit. How many pills did you take?"

"Who are you? The Red Cross?"

"How many?"

"Just three! Now let me outta here!!"

Elizabeth tried again to get past Noelle, but Noelle had a firm hold of her, and kept her under the shower.

"What did you take?"

"Only Xanax!" Elizabeth yelled. "Get the hell out of my way! Who are you anyway? A cop?"

Noelle backed away and took a towel for herself. Elizabeth took one also, and Silvi licked the wet legs of both women.

"I'm not a cop or the Red Cross," Noelle said. "*Just* three pills, and *only* Xanax, huh? Must have been having a helluva time getting to sleep."

"It's none of your business. Whose dog is this? What are you doing in my house?!"

"I am this dog's person, and you're lucky that I just happen to have some experience with overdose victims. I'm Noelle Splendor, your next door neighbor. Merry Christmas," Noelle said wryly.

"Christmas was yesterday," Elizabeth countered. "How dare you come barging into my home?! I could have you arrested for trespassing!"

"I thought there was the possibility that you were in danger, and it seemed faster to check than to go home and call 911, especially since you might have been *dying!*"

"Well, thanks a lot, and even if I were dying, that's *my* business . . . so I'll thank you very much for keeping out of it!"

Silvi licked some more water off Elizabeth's leg. The dog's caring gesture caused Elizabeth's anger to ebb. "And who's this mongrel?"

"Silvi is hardly a mongrel. Rhea Silvia is a full-bred 10 year old German Shepherd." Noelle bent down, and affectionately petted the dog on her head. "Silvi, this is . . ." Noelle looked up at Elizabeth. "What's your name anyway?"

Elizabeth narrowed her eyes, her anger starting to rise again. "My name's Elizabeth, and listen, don't expect to get all palsy walsy here. Thanks for quote 'helping' me. Now, take your dog and go home!"

"Well, excuse me," Noelle retorted. "I understand about privacy. I've had my share of privacy being invaded, so I'll be on my way. C'mon, Silvi!"

≈

7

Noelle placed the towel on the sink, and exited the bathroom. As she made her way through the littered living room, Elizabeth followed her out. Noelle peeked over her shoulder and saw Elizabeth walking slowly behind her.

"I'm sorry that I barged in, Elizabeth. I'm glad you're okay."

"Yeah... I'm okay. Thanks for..." Elizabeth interrupted herself, embarrassed about becoming too intimate. "Well, anyway, what were you doing here?"

"I moved in next door about three months ago. I've met most everybody around here except you, and Silvi comes over here everyday to pee right next to your front door."

Elizabeth laughed for the first time. "She probably smells my cat." Elizabeth's smile faded and she became sad. "Or smells what *was* my cat."

"What do you mean?" Noelle asked.

Elizabeth lost eye contact, and randomly picked up garbage. "My cat died Christmas Eve."

"Oh, I'm so sorry," Noelle said sympathetically. "How long had she lived with you?"

"Sixteen years. We'd been through a lot together."

"I'm sure. I know what that's like. Silvi turned 10 years old yesterday. She's a Christmas puppy, and we've been together since she was nine weeks old. Her dad and I had been together 20 years, and then he died five years ago."

"You mean you're a widow?" Elizabeth asked.

"Well, kind of," Noelle answered. "We never got married. I just lived with a great guy for 20 years."

"What did he die from?"

"Coronary artery disease and cirrhosis of the liver."

"Boy, I bet that's some story."

"Another time. I really did think you might have OD'd or something, and since I work in a psych ward, I kind of went into automatic."

"Where do you work?"

"At UCLA. The night shift. I just started in the fall. Listen, I don't want to keep you. I mean, it is seven o'clock Sunday morning, and

I'm just getting home. So I'm going to go. We'll talk another time, now that we've met, okay?"

Elizabeth was hesitant, but said, "Okay." She walked Noelle and Silvi to the door, and followed them as far as the archway.

Noelle stopped and turned to Elizabeth. "Would you like to come over later for dinner, or maybe go to a movie together?"

Elizabeth shrugged her shoulders. "I don't go out much."

"So I've noticed," Noelle said. "Do you go out at all?"

Elizabeth squinted in the sunlight. "You're getting personal again."

Noelle laughed. "I can see you're a tough person to get to know. "Well, we'll see you. C'mon, Silvi."

As Noelle and Silvi walked back toward their house, Elizabeth watched them wistfully. Suddenly, she called after them. "Listen, you could come back here later . . . I mean, I could clean up the place a little bit."

Noelle smiled tiredly. "Thank you, but I think I'm just going to crash. I'm sorry I busted in on you, and you don't need to be polite now. I mean . . ."

Elizabeth interrupted her. "No, it's okay. I'm not being polite. The truth is, no one's been in my place for a long time, and since you've already been inside . . . I just thought, maybe . . . nah, never mind."

"Oh, I get it," Noelle said. "Sure, I could come back later, after I've slept for a few hours."

Elizabeth got hopeful. "Maybe you want to come back right now?"

Noelle laughed. "Well, I do have to take Silvi for a walk. Why don't you come with us?"

Elizabeth shook her head and pulled back into the doorway. "No, thanks. I *really* don't go out."

"Not at all . . ." Noelle asked gently.

"No," Elizabeth answered.

"How long has it been?"

"Seven years."

"You haven't gone *anywhere* in seven years?!"

"Nope. I've worked out a whole system, and I don't have to go anywhere." Elizabeth's eyes flashed angrily. "I haven't *wanted* to go anywhere . . . that is, until yesterday . . ."

"What happened yesterday?"

"I got an invitation to a wedding."

8

"Whose wedding?" Noelle asked.

"My niece's," Elizabeth said. "My brother is this bigwig, Samuel Elias, who's inviting everybody that's anybody."

"Wow, I've heard of Sam Elias! Wasn't he voted the number one most influential person in Hollywood?"

"Yes, but that seems like a million years ago. 'The Rise and Fall of a Hollywood Power Broker' are old headlines. I'm surprised he's giving such a big reception, and that *I'm* invited, even if I did get the invitation late!"

"What do you mean late?"

"Usually wedding invitations go out six weeks ahead of time. He probably had to think about whether or not he wanted to invite me."

"Why wouldn't you be invited?"

"Noelle, I'm the crazy one in the family. The identified patient. I'm an embarrassment."

"What's the problem?" Noelle asked.

Elizabeth spoke with shame. "Do you know what agoraphobia is?"

"Yes," Noelle answered.

"Oh, yeah, right. You work in a psych ward!"

Elizabeth looked frightened for a moment. Then she laughed nervously. "Oh . . . so then you *really* know about agoraphobia, and a whole bunch of other stuff!"

"Yes, I do," Noelle said calmly. "What kind of work do you do?"

"I'm a freelance secretary, trying to be a paid screenwriter. I work at home with a computer, fax machine, email, and the U.S. mail."

"And you don't go outside at all?" Noelle asked.

Elizabeth shook her head. "Nope. To tell you why would take more than a walk with Silvi. So come back here when you're done, okay?"

Noelle thought for a beat. "So you *want* to go to this wedding?"

"Yes," Elizabeth said shyly.

"When is it?"

"A week from today."

Noelle pondered this and she suddenly smiled with an idea. "If you come with me for a walk with Silvi, I will be your date at that wedding . . . assuming you want one."

Elizabeth's eyes sparkled at the thought. "You think? Nah, I'm being silly. Seven years is a long time, but thanks anyway."

Elizabeth started to shut the door, but Noelle jumped forward to stop her. "Hey, wait a minute, Elizabeth. Sometimes you've got to go for the golden ring, you know!"

Elizabeth shook her head. She tried to push the door shut past Noelle's hand. "No, I'm sorry. I thought, just for a second, but I know I couldn't go through with it. I mean, it's a wedding for Christ's sake. Five hundred people. Bel Air Estates. I haven't seen anybody in my family for seven years!!! I was disinherited, Noelle!"

"Disinherited?! Jeez, Elizabeth, you must have a great story yourself. Just come for the walk with Silvi and me. A week is a long time away, and it would fly by. It's once we get to the wedding that will be the hard part . . . Well, never mind, let's see now . . ."

"Wait a minute," Elizabeth interrupted. "What were you going to say about the hard part?"

"Nothing," Noelle said. "The only way to get anything done is to take one step at a time. Put one foot in front of the other, and take care of what's in front of you."

"Well, then, what would we have to do first?"

"There's hair, make-up, a dress, manicure, pedicure, new shoes . . ." Noelle took a deep breath. "Damn, we better get started. The dress alone takes some people six months!"

"I hate all this," Elizabeth complained.

"All what?" Noelle asked.

"Shopping. Preparing. Traffic. It's such bullshit!"

"I can show you how it can be fun. It's only because you don't feel pretty inside, that you don't like dressing up and going out."

"Make-up can't be fun," Elizabeth said. "Women are just covering up their natural beauty."

"But weddings are events, Elizabeth, and events demand drama! Think of yourself playing Elizabeth Taylor as Cleopatra."

"Cleopatra killed herself in the end. What's so much fun about that?"

"But think of how stunningly dramatic Elizabeth Taylor looked playing with Richard Burton. God, the fun they must have had making that movie . . ."

"And the fights . . ."

"Yes, and the fights," Noelle agreed, "but at least they got to play together."

Elizabeth was puzzled. "Why do you want to do this with me, Noelle?"

Noelle thought for a beat, and tried not to show that she had filled up with tears. "Ever since my honey died . . . his name was Jimmy . . . I lost my best friend. You're my new neighbor, and maybe my new best friend. That means we have the potential to be Lucy and Ethel. Lucy wouldn't let Ethel miss her niece's wedding, now would she?"

"But you don't even really know me. Neighbors come and go. My father used to say friends are ships that pass in the night. It's family that counts."

"Yeah, and look how far that philosophy got him in his relationship with you. You said you were disinherited, right?"

"Yes. The whole thing is confusing to me. Going to the wedding is almost like sucking up to them. Like I want something from them . . . and I don't need their fucking money!"

"Well, you do want *something*! You want that word that's so popular in psycho babble . . . validation. To be lauded by peers and family is not an easy accomplishment."

"And when I give my Oscar speech, I'll thank my next door neighbor, Noelle Splendor, for insisting that I try for the golden ring."

"You go, girl!"

Elizabeth opened her front door wide. She stepped outside.

Noelle hugged her, and Silvi jumped up on both of them. Elizabeth took a few more tentative steps, and then suddenly became very nervous. "Wait a minute, Noelle. I can't do this. What was I thinking?" Elizabeth backed up a couple of steps.

Noelle grabbed Elizabeth's arm and stopped her. "Whoa, woman! What's wrong?"

"Noelle, I haven't left my house for SEVEN years! I can't, in a matter of moments, subject myself to going to a Hollywood party! Maybe if I had more time—even more time with you - just to get used to all of this . . . this . . . this space!" Elizabeth pointed in all directions.

Noelle thought for a minute. "Elizabeth, did you watch the T.V. show 'Monk?'"

Elizabeth nodded her head and laughed. "Yeah, I liked it."

"Remember that episode where his agoraphobic brother had to leave a burning house?"

"Yes," Elizabeth said solemnly. "It hit a little too close to home, because it was so compelling and believable."

Noelle put both her arms on Elizabeth's shoulders. "Listen to me. Your life is going up in smoke. You're burning it up with those drugs and alcohol in there. You've got to get out! Please, *just do it now!!!*"

Elizabeth allowed Noelle to guide her further outside. Noelle took a deep breath herself. "Elizabeth, take a deep breath. What do you smell?"

Elizabeth took that deep breath. "Christmas trees. Wow! I can smell Christmas!!"

Noelle laughed, stretching her arms. Elizabeth laughed also, stretching her own arms. They hugged each other again. Silvi ran on ahead, barking for them to come. Noelle pointed in Silvi's direction.

"Shall we?"

Elizabeth took one more deep breath. "Call me, Lizzie, okay, Noelle?"

"You got it, Lizzie. Let's go."

9

Oleo shut off the television, and stared at Elizabeth expectantly. "Well . . ."

"It's amazing how much you look like Noelle Splendor," Elizabeth said wonderingly.

Oleo smiled triumphantly. "One of my many talents is making myself look like an exact duplicate of whomever or whatever I wish."

"You mean, you could look like that rock over there?" Elizabeth asked.

In answer, Oleo disappeared, and a duplicate rock popped into being next to the rock to which Elizabeth had referred. Elizabeth was dumfounded. She ran over to the rocks, and touched the smooth stone of both of them. She said, "This woman is a piece of work!"

Elizabeth knocked on the rocks. "Hello in there? Oleo? Come out, come out, wherever you are!"

The second rock began to shimmer and glow, and then poof! It turned into Oleo, who laughed with joy. "Isn't this fun?"

Elizabeth's eyes shone with her enjoyment. "No wonder you call it the 'Fun Zone!' What's next?"

"Well, I think you're starting to get the picture. Maybe a better question is what do *you* want to do next?"

"Hmm," Elizabeth said. "This is going to require some thought. I need to know more about what my options are."

"All right," Oleo said, rolling up the sleeves of her flowing gown. Let's start by examining all the ingredients. First, there's your new friend, Noelle Splendor. What do you know about her?"

"Not much," Elizabeth answered. "With her around for moral support and transportation, I spent the last week being primped and prepped for my niece's wedding like a princess in a fairy tale, but Noelle never talked much about herself. There was that great guy she lived with for

20 years, who died from coronary artery disease and cirrhosis of the liver."

"How great could he have been if he died from those two diseases in this day and age of bypass surgery and rehab," Oleo asked.

"I never thought of that," Elizabeth said. "It was Noelle that said he was 'great.'"

Oleo had an idea. "I want you to see something." She flipped the TV to a new channel, where a pretty Catalina 36 foot sailboat gently rocked in the water. Noelle Splendor, carrying six red roses, six white lilies, and a black box lead a procession of nine people onto the vessel.

The sailboat's French Captain, Michel, started the motor, and steered her out the Marina Del Rey, California main channel into the Pacific Ocean. When they past the breakwater, the men raised sail, and the women passed around food and drink. Noelle stood at the bow, solemnly looking out to sea, holding the black box.

Michel reached his destination, and began to sail in large, slow circles. Noelle came out of her reverie, turned to Michel, and he nodded to her. "This the place."

"Thank you, Michel." Noelle turned to the small group assembled on the deck, and swallowed hard. "Jimmy's final request was to be cremated and buried at sea. Dr. James Splendor was capable of being a kind man, a sensitive man, and a mean son of a bitch. I survived living with him for 20 years . . ."

Noelle paused, studying the faces of the people that knew Jimmy the best. His son, Cory; daughter, Alison; ex-wife, Debra; sister, Marie; three best friends, John, Stan, and Michel; Michel's wife, Linda, and their son, Richard.

Noelle said, "There are no secrets about Jimmy in this group, so here goes. He. . . he threatened my life on more than one occasion. He made sweet love to me as well, and through it all, his one consistent desire was to die at sea. He accomplished his goal, but not quite the way he anticipated.

"Jimmy was drunk, standing on a dock next to his sailboat, that he called '*Feed Me*.' He was fishing, when his massive heart attack hit, and the force of it propelled him into the water. A neighbor had seen him fishing about noon. A stranger saw him face down in the water at

12:15. The stranger called 911. The paramedics tried to revive him, but they couldn't, so Dr. James Splendor was pronounced DOA in the hospital's emergency room.

"I wasn't there, and neither was our puppy dog, Silvi. Silvi had run away four days before, when Jimmy had been in a drunken rage and yelled at Silvi that she would never see me again. Silvi jumped off the boat, and ran up the dock with Jimmy cursing both of us at the top of his lungs for the whole Marina to hear.

"'Go ahead, you cunt!' he yelled. 'Leave me, just like all the rest of them have. I never met a woman who didn't leave me!'"

10

Noelle swallowed her tears, straightened her shoulders, and continued speaking. "That was the story of Jimmy's life. Beginning with his mother, who tried to abort him with a hanger and told him about it, when she herself was drunk—and ending with me, who left him 10 months ago in the lobby of a rehab facility, with both of us crying and hugging. We never got to live together again.

"When he was drunk, all women were cunts, bitches, and whores, and no one could tell Jimmy differently. He would say, 'And I'm a doctor, so I should know! After all, don't doctors know everything? Aren't doctors God compared to mortal men?'

"Jimmy could get very drunk and pissed off, when people didn't give him the respect he felt he was due for being a doctor. The fact that he was drunk and cursing them out was supposed to be ignored. He'd been abandoned by his father, who left the house when Jimmy was only two. His mother farmed out his sister, Marie, and himself to relatives. So there he was, a dyslexic, hyperkinetic little boy, before anyone knew what dyslexia and hyperkinesis were.

"His frustrated aunt and uncle sent him away to military academy when he was only seven years old, where the powers that be tried to beat him into submission, so he ran away. Jimmy fought adversity with stubbornness, a brilliant brain, and a rebellious spirit. He had a huge heart, reserved for a few choice moments, and the rest of the time, he was a depressed, ornery, sarcastic son of a bitch, who was a great cook, had a great laugh, and I loved him very much."

Noelle's voice faltered and she blinked away her tears. "I loved him, because I didn't know how to love myself, and he hugged me a lot, when nobody else was. In retrospect, we were a co-dependent, relatively dysfunctional couple, compared to what we could have been with all our education and breeding.

"While he was alive, I started having nightmares, and still have them, where I yell in my sleep with vicious anger, but during my waking hours, I tried to be tolerant and understand him. That worked most of the time, but during PMS..."

The mourners chuckled, and Noelle stood straighter. "But today isn't about me. It's about Jimmy. So, I think it's time we fulfill his last request."

Noelle held up the black box, and opened it to reveal a bag full of white sand and small rocks. She took a deep breath, opened the bag, and began to pour it overboard. She turned to Jimmy's children. "Kids, you want to help me? Cory? Alison? C'mon..."

As the children came forward, and each took their turn pouring their father's ashes into the sea, the adults threw the roses and lilies into the surrounding water. The deed was done.

Oleo turned off the television and waited for Elizabeth's reaction.

"Whew . . . I wish I knew more about what happened. There must have been so much turmoil and so much love."

"Would you like to read Noelle's diary?" Oleo asked.

Elizabeth was surprised and furrowed her brow. "What?! How could we do that? Wouldn't that be wrong? And, besides, how would you get her diary?"

Oleo bent down next to Elizabeth, and gently stroked her hair. "Dear one, I have told you. In my world, everything is possible, and in my world, there is no wrong or right. There is only what works. If it will help you to understand yourself and life a little bit more, then it will make you want to live a little bit longer. With that goal in mind, I don't think Noelle would object. She is a kind soul."

"I know she's kind," Elizabeth said, "but how would we get her diary?"

Oleo snapped her fingers, and a red leather diary appeared in her right hand. "Ask, and you shall receive."

Elizabeth shook her head in wonderment. "Oleo, you are amazing. You're sure this is okay—that Noelle wouldn't mind?"

"If you remember correctly, I do believe this is a life and death situation. We may be sitting here eating and drinking champagne in my world, but in your world, you're on your way to becoming "DOA" just like Noelle's honey, Jimmy Splendor."

Elizabeth got very sad. "I almost forgot."

Oleo handed Elizabeth the red diary. "I think it's time for you to read the story of a doctor . . ."

11

February 25th—approximately 7:30 PM.

Jimmy and I met at a community counseling center in Beverly Hills that had opened with dreams to help people, and it was a big attraction to me. I had a crush on the founder, and I was also one of his assistants.

Dr. James Splendor arrived at the clinic to do his internship for his Doctorate degree. I didn't like Dr. Splendor when I first met him.

I was, and still am to a certain degree, very shy—more so in those days—and at staff meetings, I was usually very quiet. When I did speak, I would get very nervous, my hands would sweat, and my heart would pound.

Dr. Splendor had no trouble speaking up in staff meetings. He was full of opinions, a sophisticated vocabulary, and a confidence that bordered on swaggering. I think I was even a little afraid of him, because he was confident so quickly in an environment, where it seemed to me that everyone deferred to Gene, the psychologist who ran the clinic.

Jimmy wasn't very good at deferring, and I could tell that he was older and more experienced than the other interns. He had more maturity, and he also smelled from alcohol, which came out of his pores one Saturday morning when he volunteered to paint one of the offices. He painted it with his shirt off, and I noticed he had a tattoo, "Oblivion," on his left shoulder which was a little scary to me.

I told Gene, "I think this one drinks," and Gene just laughed. I think Gene knew it long before I did. Anyway, Jimmy quickly became a fixture at the Counseling Center. He lived five minutes away by car - a 15 minute walk. He stayed late, volunteered for all kinds of extra tasks, was very handy in all kinds of areas, and had a wonderful sense of humor that he expressed freely with a deep laugh.

Over the course of the year, we became friends and I don't remember when I became attracted to him. I know I felt safe with him in a very short time, and grew to rely on him to fix just about anything—cars, phones, typewriters—if it was broken, Jimmy could fix it.

He seemed to like me and Joanie a lot. Joanie was married. I wasn't, but he treated us, Betsy, and Trudy with respect and caring. It turned out he knew Trudy from before, because she was married to his ex-brother-in-law's former business partner, but I didn't find that out until much later.

During this time, I don't remember ever seeing him drunk or even tipsy, and I only remember smelling alcohol on him that one time. We never had any disagreements, and he asked me to keep his grandfather's ring safe for him. It seemed an odd request at the time, but he said something along the lines of, that he tended to lose things, and I didn't, and if I wore it, he'd always know where it was. So I wore it on the middle finger of my left hand, because that was the only finger it felt comfortable on.

I ended up wearing that ring for the next 20 years on that same finger. I still have the ring, and later we sort of considered it as our going steady ring, and near the end, as our engagement ring. Jimmy boasted to Michel one night, that he had given me the ring deliberately, as a way of bonding me to him without my knowing it. He told me later, that since I was Gene's pet and single, that he had decided I was the "speed" of the Counseling Center. Therefore, I was the target he went after to get close to Gene, whom he needed to get his psychologist's license.

I can go two ways with this information. I can be flattered that he saw me as important enough to be the "speed," and I can also get angry at the sociopath, who was using me for what I could do for him. At the same time, my tendency is always to justify his behavior to make my anger go away, and in this instance, I also look at what people can do for me, and so I didn't consciously take offense when he first told me about being a "target." I think I felt proud at having something he wanted.

I can't remember when he gave me the first Valentine rose. It must have been the February after we'd already coupled. I do remember being very surprised and flattered, when I found the Valentine rose in a vase on my desk. No one had ever done that for me before. If he didn't have me yet, he had me after that Valentine rose.

I remember being jealous of a pretty patient, Linda something or other, when Joanie and I both noticed he had a crush on her. Anyway, he was definitely smitten by her, as he seemed to be by Gene's girlfriend, Susan, but never by me.

This used to really annoy me. I represented work - a 'target' to be worked on. These other women, he was actually attracted to, and they were women, whereas I felt like an overweight, clunky girl, who was still getting stoned a lot.

≈

12

February 26th—approximately 10:00 PM.

Jimmy told me that girls like Susan and Linda were "trouble." He said, that ever since grammar school, he had avoided girls that made him go "klablewy" inside, because once they got under your skin, you could never get them out. He felt that men grieved much harder than women, when they lost a spouse. So he protected himself from loving anyone too much, and it annoyed him that he grew fond of me.

I took it as a triumph. Coming from unrequited love with the men in my family, the fact that I was able to win Jimmy over, felt very good to me. It was bittersweet, though, when he would turn on me, and call me a cunt and a bitch at loud decibels.

It makes my chest heave right now, just thinking about it. My back hairs go up, when I hear him calling me a cunt. Every once in a while, he would apologize out of nowhere for being so fucked up, thank me for loving him, and tell me never to leave him, but this wouldn't ever be on the heels of an abusive episode—it would pop up during his depressions.

So, at the Counseling Center, we became friends. I wasn't conscious of him hitting on me. I remember one Friday night he called me to go out with him and our mutual friend Billy, but I just wanted to go to sleep early. I didn't have the hots for him at all. He said, "When you snooze, you lose," which was a frequent saying of his.

Another night, he and Billy surprised me, and came over to visit. I had done my laundry, but hadn't put my sheets back on. Billy ended up sleeping on the couch, and Jimmy and I slept on the mattress, all of us clothed. We were buddies.

Then one day it changed. My neighbor Annie and I wanted Chinese food, and we called Jimmy to come deliver it. Annie and I had already fooled around with each other behind Quaaludes and a lot of pot, and we had

also done a threesome with our Quaalude sup-
plier, Joey. So when Jimmy got there, the night
unfolded to a threesome, only Jimmy fucked
me—not Annie. She was hurt by that, and said
she didn't want to fuck him anyway. Many years
later, Jimmy said I had been his target all along,
because of my proximity to Gene, so he had
chosen that moment to consummate our almost
year old friendship. All of that sounds so harsh.

It was in late October that we coupled.
Gene was in Tahiti with Susan. I had been very
angry with Gene for going to Tahiti with "her,"
so I fucked Jimmy, and everything changed.

Right away, Jimmy's drinking became obvious, since I wasn't a drinker at all. I tried to
keep up, but it was impossible. He ordered a
Bloody Mary on our first real date, so I got one,
too, and I hated the taste of it. We were very
awkward on that first date. It was a restaurant
in the Marina—how prophetic—we began in
the Marina, and ended in the Marina. I think
he realized he'd finally gotten me, and what the
hell was he going to do with me, and I realized,
uh oh, what had I gotten myself into.

When Gene came back from Tahiti, and I
told him I had fucked Jimmy, he tried to bust

us up by threatening to fire me, if I didn't give Jimmy back his apartment key. But it didn't work, because Jimmy and I sort of became infatuated with each other—at least, I with him, and I used to tell him if he was acting, he was doing a damn good job, because it sure felt like he liked me a lot.

He didn't get drunk in front of me in those days. We had lots of sex, did lots of LSD, talked for hours on and off the phone, and generally became very close—as close as you can get when you're high on acid!

One day, Jimmy was in a hurry, ran across Robertson Blvd., and got hit by a car. He was okay, but his leg and hip were badly bruised. I spent a lot of time bringing him chicken soup, much to Gene's dismay. Gene was always coming up with places for me to go to take me away from Jimmy. On Sundays, he would call, and tell me to bring a Nate 'N Al's deli sandwich to him and Susan in Malibu. It would piss Jimmy off, that I would go, but I never felt like I had many options. Gene's alternative was that I could always choose not working for him, and he fired me a bunch of times in those days. Jeez, I'm a glutton for punishment.

So sick. Both of us were so sick. Dear God, please help me stay on the road to recovery. Help me to find the way to peace. Thank you for helping me find the road to peace and to stay on it.

13

February 27ᵗʰ—approximately 7:45 PM.

Our first Christmas together was at John and Stephanie's house. Jimmy got drunk and passed out on the floor. His friends were nice to me, and when they all went to sleep, I snuggled up next to him on the living room floor. Love is blind.

Eventually, I began to associate his getting drunk with John and Stephanie. He seemed to be normal, except when we got together with them, and they always called or stopped by. I grew to hate them, then love them, then miss them. Their marriage ended up crash diving even before ours.

Stephanie was the wild one of that couple. She and I had a few sexual encounters. One Christmas, it was just the four of us, and they all got pretty drunk. I went down on her in front of John and Jimmy, and I hadn't even had anything to drink. I was just attracted to her, and she asked me to do it, so I said, "Sure."

I was probably stoned, but maybe not. I wasn't getting stoned all day, every day, yet. That started later—after Jimmy got so physically ill—the year he had three surgeries. I don't remember exactly when the pot all day, every day, started, but I do remember feeling pretty desperate, and feeling like I had no one to talk to about it. When I was stoned, my options always seemed to increase, because my fantasies took off.

Anyway, we coupled, and at first, after Gene got used to the idea, things were okay, but then Gene started giving me problems again, jealous maybe of the time I was spending with Jimmy. Whatever the reason, Gene and I parted ways again. I went to live with Jimmy, who was still working for Gene, and I kept my apartment in the Sea Castle.

After a few months, Gene asked me to come back, and live with his new patient. I had no money, and was missing Gene, so I jumped at the chance. Jimmy was upset, but realized we needed the money, and by that time,

I was already contributing money to our living arrangement. Jimmy's mom was helping to support him, as she continued to for many years.

I was always looking at his potential, and it made me feel adequate to be helping him find that potential. After I broke away from Gene completely, I officially moved in with Jimmy. I remember feeling badly, because he kept putting off making room for my clothes. I sat down on the bed, and explained that I didn't feel welcome, because I was living out of a suitcase.

Eventually, he gave in, and I rearranged things, cleaned up, and began keeping house in the limited way that I felt comfortable, and the limited way he would allow. The garage was his domain, and no matter where we lived, we always had a million boxes full of "Jimmy stuff."

He was a constant child, and I became the parent, which was not only emasculating to him, but very draining for me. I also apparently gained a great deal of feelings of adequacy, or I wouldn't have stayed in the role so long. It's so ugly—I don't want to write anymore.

14

Elizabeth turned the page, but the next one was blank. She flipped through the diary. All the pages were blank. She looked at Oleo in surprise.

"Where's the rest? Didn't Noelle write anymore?"

"I wanted to give you a taste of intimacy," Oleo said. "One of the reasons you became an agoraphobic was because you were hurt very deeply by the people with whom you were most intimate. Now you avoid intimacy completely."

"But I want to know more. Who are Gene and Susan? What happened to John and Stephanie? Why did Noelle and Jimmy have so many problems? And where was the Sea Castle?"

Oleo laughed. "Humans have a saying that God is in the details. That's why people love gossip so much. It makes them feel connected to the inner circle."

"So how do I get the details?"

"You have to develop a relationship with Noelle, where you are willing to be intimate with your details, and she will give you her details."

"Oh, c'mon, Oleo. You said it yourself. I was hurt by the people I was most intimate with, which means my family, of course. My father was a controlling rageaholic, who used a red belt to get his way, and my mother was a shopaholic, who ignored what was happening to her children and herself by spending a bunch of his money in the stores of New York City. The world is full of money grubbing, angry sons of bitches! Why would I ever want to be intimate with anyone?"

"That's quite an indictment of the human race, Elizabeth, all based on your limited personal experiences."

"Well, they're the only experiences I've got, thank you very much!"

"You sound awfully angry."

"Why shouldn't I be angry? Life sucks, and anyone with half a brain knows it! I never understood why more people don't kill themselves!"

"Have you ever thought about why your father was the way he was, or what happened to your mother to make her so oblivious to realizing she had choices?"

"What difference does it make why they did what they did? It's not going to change anything!"

"It might make you less fearful in your own life, if you opened yourself up to the possibility that there is an alternative to being angry and defensive."

"I don't want to open up to anything. That's how people get hurt!"

"You mean, that's how you got hurt."

"Yes! I was just a little girl. I didn't deserve to be hit and left alone!"

"No one deserves to be beaten or abandoned, but it happens all the time in your world, because humans haven't yet learned the art of intimacy."

"What the hell are you talking about, Oleo?"

"There would be no war, if countries were intimate with each other. There would be no spousal abuse, if couples learned to love instead of fight. There would be no child abuse, if parents and teachers educated with patience, kindness, and tolerance instead of punishment. All of that requires the art of intimacy."

"Oleo, you sound ridiculous. What you're proposing is impractical and probably impossible. We are already too fucked up. The boundaries are already too impenetrable. Do you think the President is going to disengage the nuclear warheads, so we can be intimate with our enemies? You're living in the clouds!"

Oleo stood straight and proud. "Yes, Elizabeth, I do live in the clouds—literally! And I have a lot more freedom than any human does. You could try a little freedom—you might like it!"

Elizabeth was sullen and angry. "You make it sound so easy, but you're not human. I can't turn myself into a rock if I feel like it just by snapping my fingers."

"Oh, but you can," Oleo said.

"What are you talking about, Oleo? Watch this!" Elizabeth snapped her fingers. "Nothing! See? Nothing happens!"

Elizabeth stomped back and forth, snapping her fingers over and over.

"Allowing yourself to be an angry agoraphobic is your way of becoming a rock. You are immobile, and no one can touch you inside."

Elizabeth stopped in her tracks, mid-snap. "Go on."

"Humans live their lives almost metaphorically. They feel impotent, so they build a bomb, instead of taking the time to build their sense of emotional adequacy."

"And just how are we supposed to do that?"

"Start with understanding yourselves and each other's behavior. How much do you know about your father's childhood?"

"His mother died when he was very young, and he said his father was a mean bastard."

"Do you know the details?"

"No. He never wanted to talk about it. He said, 'What was done was done, and psychology was bullshit.'"

"So he refused to examine himself, and instead took out his rage on his family."

"Yes . . . and himself as well. He had terrible colitis. Even ended up with a colostomy bag, and doctors say that is an emotional illness, because it comes from pent up emotions."

"Would you like to know more about your father's life before you met him?"

"Sure, but he's dead!"

"In the Fun Zone, everything is possible. Come sit down. Let's watch an episode in your father's life—the story of a lawyer . . ."

Oleo turned on the television.

≈

15

Stars twinkled through a cloudy night sky over a residential neighborhood.

Elliot Elias, 35 years old, entered the front door of his family home laden with a briefcase full of reports and a stack of law books. He looked very tired.

Elliot's father, Samuel Elias, 70 years old with a white beard, sat at the supper table, reading a Bible.

Elliot was greeted by Ruth, 45, his older married sister, who attempted to take some things from him. "Oh my, Elliot, let me help you."

"Thanks, Ruth, but I think I've got it."

A book fell from the top of the stack. As Elliot bent to get it, more books fell. In disgust,

Elliot threw the rest of the books on the floor and they fell with a loud BANG!

Startled, Elliot's father looked up from his Bible. With a heavy Russian accent, he said to Elliot sharply, "Only a bum is late for the evening meal! Your sister comes to cook, and vhere are you?!"

"Listen . . ." Elliot started to say defensively, but he was interrupted by Ruth.

Under her breath, she whispered, "Be nice, Elliot."

Elliot gave her a look of annoyance, but succumbed to her wishes. "I'm sorry I'm late, Papa. I'll be right there."

"Hurry," Samuel insisted. It's almost sundown. Bedtime." Samuel mumbled his prayers softly.

As Elliot and Ruth arranged Elliot's things on the couch, there was a knock at the door. Ruth opened it to admit Jake, her husband, a man in his mid 50's. They were a pleasant looking couple, clearly comfortable with each other, as they kissed hello.

Ruth said, "I'll be just a minute, Jake."

Ruth grabbed her purse and coat from the couch. As her husband helped her put on her coat, Ruth spoke softly to Elliot. "Nathan called. He won't be here for dessert."

Elliot's face registered anger. "Again! That bastard!!"

Ruth tried to shush him, but it was too late. Samuel had heard Elliot's outburst, and said loudly, "Who are you calling a bastard in my home?"

Ruth said, "Nobody, Papa. He was just . . ."

But Samuel wouldn't let her finish. "Your brother, Nathan, vould not swear in this house!

"My brother, Nathan, does not *come* to this house!

Samuel stood up a little unsteadily. "Ruth! Tell him Nathan comes tonight!!"

Ruth regretfully shook her head. "He's not coming, Papa."

"Vhat do you mean?" Samuel demanded to know.

"You see?" Elliot said triumphantly.

Samuel ignored him. "Ruth, vhy isn't Nathan coming?"

"He had an emergency at the hospital, Papa."

Now Samuel turned to Elliot with his finger pointing up in the air. "Ach, *you* see. A doctor who helps sick people . . . not like you, a lawyer, who defends guilty ones to make money!"

Elliot answered indignantly. "Why do you always defend *him*? He gives you nothing. I give you everything!"

Samuel beat his fist against his chest. "You give me pains is vhat you give me!"

Ruth intervened, while trying to take off her coat. "All right, you two, enough. Jake and I will stay to keep the peace during dinner."

Elliot restrained her from taking off her coat, and pushed her toward the door. "No, no, we're okay. Go home with your husband."

To his father, Elliot spoke with finality. "I'm sorry, Papa. Now, sit down. I'll be going out after dinner anyway, and you'll be rid of me for a few more hours."

Samuel screwed up his face, and plopped down into his chair like a spoiled child. "In the middle of the night, who goes out? Bums, thieves, hoodlums! Who goes out after sunset?"

Elliot joined his father at the table, and began to dish out the meal. "Papa, don't start. I'll leave you some money on the table before I go."

"Ach, money again! You think giving me money makes God think you're not a bum?"

"Last week, you asked for five dollars, and I gave you ten. I can't win with you!"

"Tell me, bum, vhere do you go at such at an hour? To see a girl?"

"Yes," Elliot answered evenly.

"Vhat kind of girl sees a man in the middle of the night in the middle of the week? Only another bum!"

"Papa, stop . . ."

But Samuel was on a roll. He got louder. "You're a bum! Your customers are bums! *No vonder your mother killed herself. She knew she was raising a bum!!*"

Elliot slammed down his fork, and stood up. "That is an absolute lie, Papa! If that's how you feel, I'm leaving."

"I forbid you!"

"Don't be foolish. You can't forbid a grown man, anymore than you could forbid Mama from being so depressed."

"Foolish, he calls his father! No one treats Samuel Elias mid such disrespect! Nathan does not talk to me this way!"

"Nathan does not talk to you at all!" Elliot yelled.

Samuel yelled even more loudly. "Lies! Go lie mid the bums!

Elliot had fire in his eyes. He took a deep breath, stared intently at his father, and then flew out the front door.

≈

16

Elizabeth flipped off the television. "I can't believe it! I never knew my grandmother killed herself. What happened Oleo?"

"Esther Elias killed herself by using a gas oven. She suffered from clinical depression in an era when no one knew what the treatment was."

"How very sad. Why didn't my father tell us? I might've understood more about my own mood swings."

"He was ashamed of this dark family secret, Elizabeth. Mental illness terrifies people."

"The fight that my Dad had with his father is kind of like the one Dad and I had when I turned 18."

Oleo smiled. "Welcome to the centuries old generation gap!"

"This is the way I remember that birthday. I could see the early morning sun shimmering across the Passaic River from our bathroom window.

"Snow glistened along the banks. Icicles dripped on the bare tree limbs in our backyard. I tiptoed from the bathroom back to my bedroom, and quietly closed the door. I sat down at my desk and wrote in my diary.

Abruptly, Elizabeth's teenage diary appeared in her hands, open to the exact page. She laughed out loud. "That was a good one, Oleo!"

Elizabeth read aloud, "Today is my 18th birthday. My parents have high hopes for their princess, but Dad is 66 years old, and he said that I hurt his feelings last night when I told him that he was too old to have such a young daughter. He said I should be grateful for his wisdom, but all we do is fight."

The diary disappeared and Elizabeth clapped her hands as though trying to catch it. "Whoa! Where did it go?"

Oleo smiled benignly. "Why was your father so angry with his father?"

Elizabeth thought for a moment. "I think because my dad was trying to establish his independence . . . his own way of living, and his father was unwilling to accept it . . . in fact, forbid it."

Oleo nodded her head. "Yes. Now tell me what happened after you finished writing in your diary.

Elizabeth continued, but her brows were furrowed as she considered Oleo's words. "The morning of my birthday I was trying to avoid a fight, so I tiptoed downstairs in my faded jeans, blue sweatshirt, and sneakers. The stairs creaked under the pink shag carpeting, and I stopped, holding my breath.

"I could hear Dad snoring in the master bedroom. From the hallway, I could see into my brother's brown and white bedroom. Sammy, named for my paternal grandfather, didn't stir in his bed. Everything seemed so normal. His bookcases had *The Hardy Boys* and the complete set of *World Book Encyclopedia*. Sammy's painting of a collie hung over his dresser. I thought I was safe.

"Reaching the kitchen, I opened the refrigerator. Just as I put a package of English muffins on the counter, I was startled by Mom, who appeared in the doorway, wearing her pink robe."

"Don't eat any breakfast, honey. We'll all go out to celebrate your birthday. I woke up Daddy, and he's shaving."

"Sorry, Mom. I already made plans for breakfast. You told me that we were going out for dinner."

Mom's eyes narrowed suspiciously. "Where are you going?"

I avoided her eyes, and got busy with the English muffin. Trying to sound casual, I said, "To Mary's."

Mom assumed an accusatory tone. "You'd rather spend your birthday with your friends than your family?"

I turned to Mom with wary eyes, and measured my own words. "I want to do both."

"Who's going to be there?"

"Just some kids."

"Who?"

"Mary, Debbie. . . and Peter."

"Peter?" Mom's eyes blazed with anger. She repeated his name with venom. "Peter?!? But your father forbid you to see him!"

Oleo interrupted. "There it is! Your father tried to forbid you!"

Elizabeth flushed as she remembered the humiliation. She said, "Peter was a 19 year old child, trying to be a man, who had sort of asked me to marry him and then recanted. There was a lot of embarrassment around the event, and when my Mom brought it up, my own anger rose to match her intensity.

I put my shoulders back, stood tall, and said, "Mother, I am too old to be forbidden. I am 18 today, and I am going to see my friends. At least, they understand me. Nobody here does!"

"You stay right there!" Mom commanded. "I'm going to tell your father!"

Mom took the stairs as fast as she could, and I debated running out the front door before they could stop me. I said to myself, "This is bullshit," and suddenly I heard Dad's voice bellowing, "Elizabeth, come up here right now!"

I took the stairs two at a time.

On my way to Mom and Dad's room, I saw that Sammy was getting out of bed, probably to see the show that was about to happen. He was still dutifully living at home to save his money.

I entered my parents' lavender bedroom with its chandelier, providing the light to set the stage. Dad stood at his bathroom door in his boxer shorts, shaving cream on half of his face, his razor in one hand, and a towel in the other.

Mom righteously sat on the bed, front and center, to watch the carnage.

Dad was already incensed. "I thought I told you not to see Peter anymore!"

My stubbornness kicked in. "I won't be told what to do!"

"As long as I'm paying your bills, you'll do what I tell you to do!"

"I won't!"

"If you insist on seeing that bastard, I'm not going to pay for any more fancy college in Boston."

"I don't care."

"I'll keep you at home! You'll work in my office during the day, and stay with us every night!"

"I'll run away!"

"I'll lock you in your room!"

"Then I'll leave now!"

Dad walked to his dresser, opening the drawer that held the red belt, his favorite method of discipline. I backed up. Mom's eyes glazed over. Sammy appeared in the hallway behind me in his underwear.

Dad pulled out his weapon, and unfurled it, placing the buckle with the tip. "I thought only Samuel had to learn the hard way. I can see now I was wrong."

I said, "Dad. . ." but he was over the edge. He snapped the belt across my thighs. For a moment, I was in shock, and stood there unable to move.

He yelled, "*Tell me, you are going to stay!*"

I yelled back, "*No!*"

Dad whipped the belt across my legs, this time yelling simultaneously. "TELL ME, YOU ARE GOING TO STAY!!"

I screamed, "NO! I WON'T!!"

Frantically, he began trying to beat me into submission. I pushed past him, running into the hallway, and dodging past Sammy. I ran down the stairs, hearing Dad's threat, "If you leave this house, I'll disinherit you!"

17

Elizabeth took a deep breath.

Oleo said, "And that brings us to Sammy..."

"Who I don't know much about these days, except what I've read in the newspaper," said Elizabeth. "The Indian Chief and I stopped speaking after my parents' wills were read, and he decided to uphold their decision. That was seven years ago."

Oleo sighs. "Here's where the tricky part begins. We'll have to be invisible in your brother's surroundings for a little while. We have to do some preliminary work to catch you up on who Sam really is, and when we get to the part where you're about to get shot, you can elect to stop the action, and pop back into your world."

"You mean, that's where I get to alter my future?"

"Yes, but first we have to update you on your brother, who ironically enough, just like you, is a forgotten person."

"How can that be?" asked Elizabeth.

"Sam has lost his way, and feels very alone in the world. There are people who dislike him, are jealous of him, and revel in his misfortune. He is enduring a prolonged emotional beating that many think he deserves."

"Does he deserve it?" Elizabeth asked.

"Karma is a funny thing," Oleo answered. "One of the great unanswerable questions. Why don't we peek in on the story of an Indian Chief, and you decide for yourself."

18

The Brentwood estate of Samuel Elias was set behind gates on one of those hidden streets with enormous beautiful trees. Elizabeth and Oleo popped into view next to a huge piece of metal sculpture. Elizabeth did a double take. "Whoa, I didn't expect to come here this second! I thought you said we'd be invisible." She glanced around nervously.

"We can be seen and heard only by each other."

Elizabeth was incredulous. "Are you sure?"

Oleo nodded wryly. "Trust me. I've been traveling a long time. Let's enter through the library." Oleo glided over the grass through an open patio door. Elizabeth quickly followed.

Inside, sat one of the finest private art collections in the world. Everything ranging from

Chinese furniture and ceramics to contemporary sculpture and modern paintings. Elizabeth commented sarcastically, "Samuel always wanted the best of everything."

Suddenly, the man himself entered, touching fabrics and pieces of art as he walked through the room. Elizabeth froze at the sight of her compactly built brother. Oleo reassured her in a normal tone of voice. "No fear. Remember, he can't see or hear us."

Elizabeth cautiously watched her brother as he breathed deeply. He slowly took in the sights and feel of his library, getting comfort from his art collection.

"Sammy looks tired," Elizabeth whispered.

Oleo answered sternly, "Stop whispering. It's time for you to quit pussy footing around. If you want to change the course of your life, you have to behave like a champion instead of a scared rabbit."

Elizabeth stood straighter, clearing her throat. "You don't mince words, do you, Oleo?"

"The human life span is too short, Elizabeth. Your brother is thinking about his daughter's upcoming wedding, and he's worried about several things. One looming item totally out of his control is that you're coming."

"But he invited me!"

"He didn't think you'd come."

"Great. Thanks for telling me, Oleo."

"Rigorous honesty with yourself will save you, Elizabeth. Right now, it seems to Samuel like everything is out of his control, but you, in particular, aren't even in his ballpark."

"What do you mean?" asked Elizabeth.

"His sources have told him that you're drinking too much, smoking dope and cigarettes, taking sleeping pills, and don't come out of your house."

"Who the hell are his sources?"

"A man with his connections has eyes everywhere. He knows you're capable of any kind of acting out behavior, and he was against inviting you to the wedding."

Elizabeth sniffed the air contemptuously. "Then why did he?"

"Because his daughter Emma implored him to invite her only aunt, eccentric though her aunt may be."

"I always sent her fun birthday presents."

"Yes, you did," said Oleo kindly, "and Samuel has an extremely soft spot in his heart for Emma. He relented at the last minute."

Samuel paused in front of a wall full of family photographs. Oleo lead the way for her and Elizabeth to walk up behind Samuel. He reached out to touch a series of pictures of a baby, a little boy, an adolescent, and finally a teenager, sporting purple hair, a pierced nose, and proudly flaunting a pierced nipple.

"That's my nephew, Bobby. He turned 18 this year."

Oleo filled in the gaps for Elizabeth. "Bobby is completely beyond Sam's reach emotionally. He's intent on trying every drug humans have discovered or invented, and has been invading Sam's bar with a frequency that is very troubling to his father. In Sam's high profile fast lane life, he has watched too many children of famous people come to unhappy endings."

Elizabeth nodded her head. "The media is full of the horror stories."

"Unfortunately, your nephew has a propensity for violence as well."

"What does that mean?"

"He has what's known as Intermittent Explosive Disorder."

"Oh, I get it. So he fights a lot with Sam."

"Yes. He fights with everyone, and the drugs just exacerbate it."

"How is Sam helping him?"

"Right now, Bobby doesn't want any help."

"But it's his son! Sam can afford to get Bobby the finest doctors in the world. Put him into one of those rehab places, and set him up with a shrink."

"Bobby has to want residential treatment, unless, of course, now that he's turned 18, he gets incarcerated for his illegal behaviors."

"Prison isn't going to help!"

"How would you handle the situation?"

"With patience, kindness and tolerance."

"It didn't do you much good, Elizabeth."

"What are you talking about?"

"Your friend Noelle gave you exactly those things this whole week before the wedding, and you still ended up with a bullet in your brain."

"That's different."

"Is it? Have you remembered yet what led up to you getting shot?"

"No. I'm thinking maybe I drank too much and I blacked out sometime during the wedding. I'd been having a lot of blackouts before I met Noelle and stopped drinking for that one week."

"Why didn't you stop drinking all those years?"

"I tried," Elizabeth said with shame, "but it's not so easy."

"Exactly. You needed help, and you were unwilling to surrender to those who could help you. Your nephew Bobby is in the same predicament. He thinks he knows it all—typical for a human 18 year old."

"What about Sammy?" Elizabeth retorted. "He always thought he knew it all!"

"Yes, and Samuel has been through a lot these last years, especially when he had to sell his struggling management company. Sam has traveled quite a road from the mailroom to super agent to a falling Hollywood power broker."

"What's next for him?"

"He will always rebound, and he knows that a lot of old friends, enemies and just plain curious relatives will be attending Emma's wedding."

"Certainly, I can't be his most pressing worry."

"No, you're not. The person Samuel is most interested in seeing is Barry Levine."

"Wasn't that his business partner in the talent agency?"

"His former business partner. Their breakup was devastating for all concerned, and Barry is the one person in the world who knows Samuel better than anyone, even his wife."

Sam moved to another wall, full of photographs with him and Barry cavorting with different celebrities. The Oscars, the Emmy's, the Tony's, premieres, restaurants, tennis, golf. The pictures seemed endless.

"They did it all together," Elizabeth said. "They were probably more like brothers than Sam and I ever felt related to each other."

"Samuel needs to make peace with Barry," Oleo said, "and he knows it's not going to be easy."

"From what I've read, Barry has plenty of reasons to be pissed off," said Elizabeth.

"Yes. Not the least of which was when Samuel bought some Malibu property, that Barry wanted very badly for his wife, and speaking of wives, look who's here."

19

"Oh my," Elizabeth exclaimed. "Jenny looks great!"

Jenny Elias made her entrance, wearing expensive riding clothes. Two dogs happily trailed behind her, one carrying a tennis ball. "Hi, Sam, what are you doing in here?"

Samuel smiled, seeing his radiant wife. "Hi, Jenny."

"Emma is getting nervous bride's jitters. She's in her room dressing, and she sent me to find her Daddy to give her a good luck kiss. You better get going, Sam. I'm going to get in the shower."

"Jenny, you asked me what I was doing in here."

"Oh yes, I did. I have so many things on my mind, and I can't remember any of them from one moment to the next. This library is so lovely. I feel better every time I spend time in it.

"That's why I'm here."

Jenny put her arm on her husband's shoulder. "What's the matter, Sam? Father of the Bride feeling old and blue?"

Samuel pointed to all the pictures on the walls. "So many memories, Jenny. One day, Barry and I were just bullshitting about starting our own talent agency, and that little pebble turned into a behemoth."

"Artists Creative Management really did take on a life of its own, didn't it, Sam?"

"Suddenly, we had partners, and the mega star clients kept coming. The deals got bigger. Our power increased. . . and then one day, I came crashing down."

"Sam, don't think of it that way."

"At least, Barry is Vice Chairman of Atlas Studios' parent company, but I . . . I think I'm finally going under."

Jenny moved closer to her husband, trying to cheer him. "You are being ridiculous, Samuel Elias. We are about to throw a lavish wedding for our beautiful daughter who's head over heels in love with a wonderful man from a delightful family."

"Yes, her life will be good."

Jenny stamped her foot. "And so will ours, Sam. We have our health, and we certainly have plenty of money."

"It's not the money, Jenny. It's the respect for me that's not there anymore. I've burned too many bridges, waged too many battles, and the town is glad to see me fall."

Jenny touched Sam's face. "Remember how I use to complain to you, asking when was it my turn? You were up before dawn to do your martial arts. You'd go to the office early. The kids and I spent our days waiting for you, and you'd come home so very late. I spent more hours waiting for you in restaurants than I did eating in them! Sometimes I felt so lost."

"Well, now I'm the lost one. Even having a closet fall of Armani suits isn't going to solve this problem."

The couple embraced.

≈

20

Oleo sat in a comfortable chair. "Jenny was very patient with Samuel, and she ended up growing into her own position of power as a goldfish in a pool of sharks. She was on the Boards of two hospitals, and Sam had to write a letter to one of them to back off when they wanted her to choose."

Elizabeth sat opposite Oleo. "What was she going to do, carry state secrets to the hospital board meetings? I've always thought if Samuel hadn't been so power hungry, their lives would've been more emotionally fulfilling, but as I sit here watching them together, I think they really do like and respect each other."

Samuel walked to his desk and sat down. "Jenny, do you remember the ACM Christmas party we threw the year the Japanese bought Atlas Studios?"

"How could I forget? All by yourself, you earned $60 million, and squandered quite a bit of it on gifts for us."

Samuel stood and started pacing. "Everybody made money back then. Hell, William Morris was taking huge packaging fees from shows like "Cosby" and "Barney Miller." Once the shows went into syndication, the agency was getting $300, $400, even $500 million. William Morris had dedicated their new building to Bill Cosby, and all that money and power brought me to my knees."

"Sam, don't do this to yourself. We have to move forward."

"But, Jenny, I started so many wars. The casualties have been endless and I am so tired."

"Are you too tired to be angry?"

"I think so. . . even Lew Wasserman is dead. The guy who created Universal Studios. That makes me feel old and scared. Death is the great leveler."

"Samuel, stop it! We all march to the same destination, no matter what role or roles we played while we're here."

"Jenny, I remember telling Barry and the other guys that Wasserman's friend, Joe Evans, was too old to run Atlas Studios, and that I should be head of Atlas. They laughed at me. I hated being laughed at. And now so many others are laughing."

Jenny grabbed Samuel and put his face between her hands. "I won't stand for this self pity. History will write about you as a great visionary, and right now, your daughter is waiting for you."

Samuel was sheepish. "Jenny, I'm sorry for all the times I kept you waiting."

"We're partners, Samuel. We do whatever it takes to make things work."

Jenny and Sam hugged tightly, and walked out of the room arm in arm.

Elizabeth turned to Oleo, "I didn't know he was capable of an apology."

"Are you capable?" Oleo asked.

Elizabeth narrowed her eyes. "What do you mean?"

Oleo smiled gently. "You might want to think about your part in the breach with him."

"But. . ."

"No buts. Mature creatures take responsibility for their actions, and always remember what Mae West said, 'It takes two to get one in trouble.'"

"I'll think about it," Elizabeth said.

Oleo put her arm through Elizabeth's. "Let's go reconnoiter the wedding!"

≈

21

Elizabeth and Oleo exited the library, and Oleo lead them to the elaborately decorated backyard. In one area was an elegant "*chuppah,*" a magnificent embroidered canopy under which the young Jewish couple would be married.

Elizabeth's breath was taken away. "Oh my, Oleo, will you look at that *chuppah*? It's stunning! And so many flowers!!"

"Your brother has spared no expense."

"I wish he loved me as much as he loves Emma."

"What makes you think he doesn't love you?"

Elizabeth was surprised at Oleo's response. "It's obvious, isn't it? If he loved me, he would've given me my half of the estate, even though Mom and Dad didn't want me to have anything."

"Elizabeth, what do you think is truly the reason your parents didn't want you to have any money or any of their possessions?"

"I think they never got over thinking of me as the baby."

"Why is that?"

"Because I was the youngest."

"Think harder, Elizabeth. What was the behavior that created problems?"

"I thought it was because I never got married."

"And why didn't you get married?"

"I never met the right guy."

"What was your criteria for the 'right guy?'"

"He had to like to get high for one thing. I love pot."

"Do you think that a mature man is going to want an immature woman?"

"What's that supposed to mean, Oleo?"

"You started smoking marijuana in high school, and graduated to being dependent on it 24 hours a day, seven days a week in college."

"So what? It's just pot."

"You didn't stop after college. You just got better quality dope as you entered the work force."

"Yes, Oleo, and your point is?"

"It affected all areas of your life, particularly your emotional and intellectual growth."

"So what? I never wanted to be a conservative uptight adult."

"I think your parents realized that, and were unwilling to entrust the fruits of their lifetime of effort to someone they perceived as mentally ill."

Elizabeth was outraged. "Listen, I started isolating because I got so pissed off at everyone, and then . . . well, after Mom and Dad died, and they wrote that awful will, and then Sammy upheld it . . . well, I just decided to say 'fuck you' to everybody!"

"Elizabeth, I think you started to say 'fuck you' to everybody long before your parents died."

"As soon as I got into high school, they didn't like anything about me. Not my clothes, my friends, my boyfriends, my politics, my makeup—nothing! By that time, they loved everything about Sammy. He could do no wrong. Marijuana made it all hurt less. When I was stoned, I didn't care so much if they didn't love me. I daydreamed a lot about showing them how wrong they were."

Oleo headed toward the driveway. Elizabeth watched her go in dismay. "Where are you going, Oleo? Are you going to abandon me like my family did?"

"Come with me. I want you to watch Sam interact with Emma, so that you can see his soft side." Oleo snapped her fingers, and both women disappeared, only to reappear inside Emma's bedroom.

≈

22

Samuel stood in the doorway, silently watching his daughter put the finishing touches on her makeup. She was in a robe and as lovely as a young Audrey Hepburn.

Emma tilted the angle of the mirror to look at the back of her hair, and she saw her father. "Hi, Dad. I'm almost ready to put on the dress."

"You already look beautiful, Emma. I'm going to miss you."

Emma hugged Samuel tightly. "Don't be silly. I'm not going anywhere."

Samuel smiled at his daughter. "You have no idea where you're going, honey."

"What do you mean?"

"Just that life holds more surprises than you can imagine. Mom said you wanted to see me."

Emma moved toward the window, nervously adjusting the belt on her robe. "Daddy ... I ... I ..."

"Emma, whenever you call me 'Daddy,' you want something."

Emma was embarrassed. "I don't want your feelings to be hurt."

"Just say it, sweetie."

"I don't want you to ever stop loving me."

Samuel laughed, joining Emma at the window. "Emma, that is the last thing you need to worry about. Why in the world would you say such a thing?"

Elizabeth whispered to Oleo. "I guess I'm not the only one!"

Oleo put her finger to her mouth and said, "Shhh, I want you to hear this."

Emma continued, "Sometimes I think you've stopped loving Aunt Lizzie, and she's your *sister*, Daddy!"

Samuel turned from Emma in frustration.

Elizabeth said, "This is going to be good."

Samuel tried to be kind. "Emma, please. Against my better judgment, I've invited her to the wedding, only because you pleaded so well on her behalf, but don't try to meddle in how I feel about her. Don't compare yourself to her."

"But, Daddy, she chose a lifestyle that's different than ours, and you don't want anything to do with her. What happens if one of those surprises life throws at us is that my husband and I choose a lifestyle that's different than yours and Mom's. Will you stop loving me?"

"First of all, Emma, I haven't stopped loving Elizabeth. How I feel about her is complicated to explain, and we have a history together that's entirely different than my history with you. Second of all, your brother has chosen a lifestyle that's different than your mother's and mine, and I haven't stopped loving him."

"Yes, but you don't like him very much."

"Not liking someone's behavior is entirely different than not loving them. If it will ease your mind to hear it, I love your brother, I love your aunt, and I will never stop loving you, no matter what you do."

Emma went into her father's arms. "You're sure, Daddy?"

Samuel stroked her hair. "I'm sure, baby. I'm sure."

Elizabeth was amazed. "Oleo, Sammy said he loves me."

Oleo smiled. "Yes, dear, he did. Now, let's go."

"Where are we going this time?"

"Toward your future, Elizabeth. Your nephew will be pulling into the driveway by the time we get there. I think his behavior will teach you about your own. Let's go."

≈

23

Just as Elizabeth and Oleo popped outside, a brand new red Corvette roared into the driveway past the Valet setting up for the wedding guests. Bobby Elias pulled up in front of one of the four garages and parked. He turned off the motor, but left his radio blasting. Bobby checked to make sure no one was watching him, and bent over inside the car, instead of getting out of it.

"What's he doing?" Elizabeth asked Oleo.

Oleo walked to the car and stood next to the driver's window. Elizabeth followed, and her eyes opened wide as she saw Bobby snorting white powder from a little mirror. "Uh oh. Cocaine is going to get Bobby into trouble!"

Oleo nodded. "That's not the only thing."

Bobby licked his paraphernalia, put it away, and pulled a joint out of his pocket. He lit it and smoked it, while checking his rear view mirror and over his shoulder. Bobby tapped his steering wheel in time to the radio's blaring music.

Elizabeth was worried. "This is not good."

Oleo said, "There's more."

Bobby opened the glove compartment, and pulled out a small gun, which he put into his pocket.

Elizabeth cried out in alarm. "Oh my God, a gun! Oleo, Bobby has *the* gun! This is very, very bad. We must stop him!"

Suddenly, three more cars followed each other into the driveway. The Valet opened the first car door, and the Rabbi stepped out. Another Valet opened the second car, and Sam's elderly Uncle Nathan and his family emerged. Right behind them was the car carrying the bridegroom with his family.

Bobby beeped his horn several times, as he stubbed out the joint, and jumped out of the car yelling, "It's party time!"

Inside Samuel and Jenny's bedroom, the couple was just finishing dressing. Samuel heard his son's horn and his yelling, and opened the bedroom window. He waved to everyone, and softly said, "Jenny, that kid is capable of ruining this whole thing."

Jenny patted her hair one last time, and headed for the hallway. "Think positive, Sam."

≈

24

Elizabeth paced nervously. "What are we going to do, Oleo? The boy has the gun!"

Another car pulled into the driveway. This time, it was Noelle who got out of the driver's side, and a frightened Elizabeth who got out of the passenger seat.

Oleo turned to Elizabeth, standing next to her. "There you are."

Elizabeth's jaw had dropped open. "And there you are!"

"It's Noelle."

"It's us!!"

"To avoid confusion," Oleo said, "We will refer to you as Elizabeth, and your earthly counterpart as 'Lizzie,' since that's what everyone will call her."

"Except Sammy."

Oleo smiled. "I think you're in for some surprises."

As Lizzie tried to stay awkwardly close to Noelle, Bobby ran up to his aunt, lifted her off the ground, and swung her around in a big hug. "Aunt Lizzie, you made it!"

Lizzie was embarrassed in front of all the people. "Yes, Bobby, now put me down, honey."

The stoned Bobby was in his own world. He practically dropped Lizzie to the ground, and ran over to his great uncle. "Hey, Uncle Nathan, how they hangin'?"

Lizzie whispered to Noelle. "Bobby is so big! My Uncle Nathan looks so old!! Noelle, this was a terrible idea. I want to go home!"

Noelle patted Lizzie's back. "Steady, Lizzie. We can do this."

Lizzie edged back toward the car. "I don't think so, Noelle."

"Be brave, Lizzie. Look, your Uncle Nathan is waving to you."

Lizzie waved back. Noelle steered them toward Lizzie's uncle, and then suddenly Samuel and Jenny came out the front door. Lizzie froze.

As Elizabeth witnessed all the action apprehensively, she said to Oleo, "What do we do?"

"We watch the events unfold, Elizabeth. When you're ready, you tell me, and I will pop you inside Lizzie to try and change your destiny."

"You're kidding, right, Oleo?"

"Have I kidded you so far?"

Elizabeth shook her head no. She tentatively walked closer to Lizzie and Noelle.

Lizzie's eyes were focused on her brother and sister-in-law. Sammy and Jenny were being the consummate hosts.

Bobby grabbed his future brother-in-law, and pulled him to say hello to Lizzie. "David, this is my Aunt Lizzie."

Lizzie shook hands with David and introduced Noelle. "Nice to meet you, David. This is my neighbor and good friend, Noelle Splendor." They all shook hands.

Lizzie and Sam made eye contact. For a moment, neither reacted. Noelle noticed that they'd spotted each other, and she nudged Lizzie. "Go say hello to Sam."

Lizzie was half afraid, half angry. "Let him come say hello to me."

"Meet your brother halfway, Lizzie."

Lizzie looked at Noelle, seeing the kindness in her eyes. She nodded in agreement, and walked toward Samuel. Samuel did indeed meet her halfway, but they stiffly exchanged a superficial hug.

Lizzie said, "Hi, Sammy."

"Hello, Elizabeth," Sam responded.

Bobby piped up. "Come on, Dad, call her Lizzie, like you did when you were kids."

Jenny joined them. "Yes, Sam." She hugged her sister-in-law. "Welcome, Lizzie. I'm so glad you could join us."

Lizzie was a little dazed at all the activity. "Hi, Jenny. I'm not used to so many people."

"That's all right, dear. As soon as you eat something, you'll feel better. Introduce me to your friend."

"Noelle, this is my sister-in-law, Jenny, and my brother, Sammy."

They shook hands. Other guests arrived, and a servant entered with an announcement. "It's time for the wedding. Would everyone please take your seats outside."

Everybody moved their way through the house into the backyard, where the wedding was going to take place.

25

The wedding was pulled off without a hitch. As the guests circulated, Lizzie got separated from Noelle, and headed right for the bar. She found Bobby already there.

Lizzie gulped her first drink, and immediately ordered a second, drinking it very fast as well.

Bobby was impressed. "Hey, Aunt Lizzie, you know how to slam 'em!"

Lizzie nodded as she drank, trying to make her anxiety disappear.

Noelle caught up to them, "Lizzie, maybe you should slow down."

Lizzie was annoyed. "Leave me alone, Noelle. Everything is fine."

Bobby swallowed a shot of tequila, licked his lips, and said, "Yeah, Noelle, everything is just fine. Hey, Mr. Bartender, give us a couple of more shots of tequila."

Elizabeth and Oleo stood nearby. Elizabeth said, "I remember this part. I was intent on getting drunk as fast as I could."

"So was Bobby," added Oleo. "Are you ready to take control of your body?"

Elizabeth shook her head. "No way. I get nauseous just thinking about it. I can't remember anything that happened after this, except getting into a bed."

"This is your chance, Elizabeth. You can stop yourself from getting into a drunken blackout and getting shot in the brain. You know that Bobby has the gun."

"I don't have the slightest idea what to do differently."

"Wing it, dear one. That's what life is all about."

"But where will you be, Oleo?"

"Wherever you need me to be."

"How will you know if I need you?"

"I know everything, remember?"

Elizabeth took a deep breath. "Ok, go for it, Oleo. Do your stuff."

Oleo snapped her fingers and the two women disappeared.

26

The Bartender served two shots of tequila to Bobby and Lizzie. Bobby lifted up his to clink glasses with Lizzie.

Lizzie picked up her drink, and a strange look passed over her face. Elizabeth had come back into her body, and she moved her shoulders and neck, as though readjusting to the fit. Elizabeth glanced at Noelle, who had a worried expression, not knowing if Elizabeth would continue drinking. Elizabeth slowly put her glass down. Noelle breathed a sigh of relief.

"I think I'll pass on this one, Bobby. You might want to do the same."

"What's the matter, Aunt Lizzie? Can't hold your liquor?"

"No, Bobby, I don't think I can."

"Well, I can! I'll have yours."

As Bobby reached for Elizabeth's drink, she put her hand on his, trying to stop him, but Bobby was much too fast and downed it immediately. He coughed as the liquid burned his throat.

Elizabeth took his arm. "Come with me, Bobby."

Bobby shook her off. "No. I'm fine."

Elizabeth turned to Noelle. "Will you help me, Noelle?"

"Sure, what do you want me to do?"

"Help me get Bobby into the library."

As the two women steered Bobby away from the bar, he resisted loudly. "Hey, what do you think you're doing? Leave me alone!"

People turned around to look at them.

Elizabeth whispered, "Bobby, I know you've got a gun in your pocket."

Bobby was stunned. "What?! How?!"

Elizabeth continued. "Let me take you to a safe place, where we can talk about it quietly."

Bobby was angry. "I have nothing to talk about, especially with you!"

"It doesn't matter what your father has told you about me. What does matter . . . what's important . . . is that I love you. Please come with Noelle and me into the library."

Bobby saw the sincerity in his aunt's eyes, and he allowed himself to be led away from the wedding party into the library.

Unfortunately, when they opened the door, it was not a safe place to be alone. Samuel was there, talking with Barry Levine, his former partner, and the two men were startled to have company.

≈

27

Bobby broke the grasps of Elizabeth and Noelle. "You set me up, Aunt Lizzie. It's *not* safe in here. My father was right. You can't be trusted!" Bobby slammed the door of the library, backed into a corner, and shakily pulled the gun out of his pocket. He aimed it at one person after another.

Samuel was astonished and frightened. "My God, Bobby, what are you doing? Put that gun down immediately!"

"I'm not a minor anymore, Dad. You can't tell me what to do, and I know how to protect myself!"

Elizabeth tried to calm him. "Bobby, I didn't know your father and Barry Levine would be in here. I really thought it would be safe for us to talk."

"You're a liar, Aunt Lizzie. You don't care about anyone, and that's why you abandoned us all these years!"

Barry Levine gently spoke up. "Bobby, please listen to us. You don't want to hurt anyone. Whatever it is, we can work it out."

"Bullshit, Uncle Barry. I know all your agent tricks. You and my father made a fortune negotiating deals, and then you fucked each other anyway. None of you can be trusted!"

Before anyone else could respond, the door opened, and Jenny entered with Uncle Nathan. She said, "Come on, Uncle Nathan, I can't wait to show you what Samuel has done with the library."

Jenny and Uncle Nathan stopped in their tracks, when they saw what was occurring. Uncle Nathan took Jenny's arm.

"Bobby, honey, what are you doing?" asked Jenny. "Is that a real gun? Is it loaded?!"

"Of course, Mother! I need it for protection."

"Bobby, listen to me," Elizabeth said. "I didn't abandon the family. I thought they abandoned *me*, and I was just retaliating, but I hurt everyone, *including myself*. Don't you do the same thing!"

"You're crazy, Aunt Lizzie. Dad's been telling us that for years, and that's why Grandma and Grandpa cut you out of their wills!"

"Bobby, I'm not crazy. I have severe depression, just like your great-grandmother did. That's why she killed herself!"

"You're lying again. Tell her Dad. She's a liar!"

"Lizzie, Grandmother didn't kill herself. She died when gas accidentally escaped from the stove."

"No, Sammy. I know that's what we were told all these years, but it's not what really happened. Uncle Nathan, do you know the truth?"

The elderly Uncle Nathan was shaking. He looked from one relative to the other, not knowing where to begin. "Elizabeth, I . . . I promised."

"What are you talking about, Uncle Nathan? Tell us!" Samuel demanded.

"I can't, Samuel. I promised I would never tell the family secret."

"Please, Uncle Nathan, you must!" Elizabeth said. "If Bobby and the rest of them can understand that emotional illness runs in families, you will save Bobby's life . . . and maybe mine, too . . . *You have to break the code of silence!*"

Uncle Nathan gazed at the floor, too ashamed to make eye contact. "You have to realize that my mother gave birth to seven children. Two of them died in childbirth. That, in and of itself, is heartbreaking. My father was a dairy farmer, but there was no money to be had, so we were very poor. The winters in New Jersey were so bitter, and we didn't have heat like you do today."

Uncle Nathan looked from one person to another with pleading eyes. "You have to understand how poor we were. When our shoes got holes in them, all Mama could do was put in cardboard soles, and we had to walk through the snow to get to school. It was awful. Worst of all, was that my father was no comfort to anyone. He was an Orthodox Jew, who buried his head in the Bible, whenever he wasn't working. He thought women and children were useless, and didn't have a kind word for any of us."

Samuel said, "Dad told me that he and Grandfather had a lot of fights, but he said that Grandfather always liked you, Uncle Nathan."

"It took a long time for that to happen. Papa wanted a doctor in the family more than anything, and I did that for him. He didn't trust lawyers, and he never forgave your father for becoming one."

Elizabeth approached Bobby, who had let the gun point toward the floor. "You see, Bobby, there's hope for all of us."

Bobby was startled, and raised the gun again, aiming it back and forth between Elizabeth and Samuel.

"Just wait a minute, Aunt Lizzie. That explains our family history, but it doesn't justify yours and Dad's behavior."

"What do you mean, Bobby?" Samuel asked.

"You didn't have to ostracize Aunt Lizzie, just because Grandpa and Grandma did. You're an educated, wealthy man. You didn't start out poor like Grandpa did, and everybody knows more today about psychology and all that stuff . . . And look at what happened to you and Uncle Barry, and Artists Creative

Management. You were partners! You knew each other so well, and had your eyes on each other all the time, and you still took each other for a ride! I can't trust anybody, especially my family!!"

Samuel moved toward Bobby. "Son, that's not true."

"Yes, it is!" Bobby cocked the gun, and shot it at his father.

≈

Elizabeth jumped in front of Samuel, taking the bullet herself. The force of the shot caused her to fall to the floor.

Barry grabbed Bobby, raising the arm that was holding the gun to the ceiling. Samuel grabbed Bobby's other arm, and took the gun from him. Jenny and Noelle ran to Elizabeth.

Uncle Nathan could hardly bend down, but his old bones made it to examine Elizabeth.

At the sound of the gunshot, Emma, David, and several other guests came running into the library.

Jenny called out, "Emma, call 911!"

Emma rushed to the phone.

Uncle Nathan said, "The bullet's in her shoulder, but she's so fragile, that she's losing a lot of blood."

Noelle said, "Dr. Elias, I've had some medical experience. Let us help you get her onto the desk, and we can try to take out the bullet, while we're waiting for the paramedics."

"Yes," said Uncle Nathan. "Jenny, get some tweezers fast!" Jenny ran out of the room.

Elizabeth could see the people milling around her. In her mind, she thought, "Where are you, Oleo?"

Oleo appeared, but only Elizabeth could see her. "I'm right here, dear."

"I need you, Oleo."

"You're doing fine, dear one."

"I don't want to die, Oleo."

"Then you are no longer a forgotten person, Elizabeth. I can go on to the next item in my treasure hunt, and you can go on with your life."

"But I have a bullet in me."

"Yes, dear, but it's in your shoulder, not your brain."

Jenny ran back into the room, and handed the tweezers to Uncle Nathan. He and Noelle got to work.

Oleo continued. "You will be fine, Elizabeth. There's only one thing left to do."

"What's that?"

"Make peace with your brother."

"He still owes me a lot of money."

"He doesn't owe you any money, Elizabeth. No one owes anybody anything. Everything is a choice, and no one is entitled to anything. Perhaps one day, Samuel will choose to share what he has with you. Until then, forget about the money. Love is the only thing that matters. Goodbye, dear."

"Oleo, wait!"

"Yes, Elizabeth."

"Thank you . . . thank you for giving me my life back."

"You gave it to yourself, dear one. It takes a strong woman to be so brave . . . and remember, always try to live in the Fun Zone!" Oleo disappeared.

Elizabeth yelled in pain. Uncle Nathan held up the bullet for everyone to see. They all cheered.

Samuel turned to Bobby and Barry. "Son, will you please stay here with Uncle Barry?"

Bobby nodded, but said nothing. His eyes were glazed over. Samuel touched his shoulder. "We can help you, Bobby, as long as you let us."

Bobby said, "Okay, Dad."

Samuel asked Barry, "Do you have him, Barry?"

"Yes, Sam. I've got your back. I always did."

The partners smiled at each other with the fondness they knew so many years ago.

Samuel approached Elizabeth, and stroked her hair. "Why did you do that, Lizzie? You could have died, trying to save me."

Elizabeth smiled at him with the strength she had left. "That's what you do in a family, Sammy. You look out for each other."

"Thank you, Lizzie. I'm sorry that I . . . that I . . . didn't love you enough."

"Me, too, Sammy. I wish I'd been healthier, and knew how to love you and the family more."

The paramedics arrived. People parted to make way for them and their equipment, and they started to work on Elizabeth.

≈

29

Oleo turned the pages of a wedding album, seeing Elizabeth with a sling over her arm in lots of pictures with the bride, groom and their respective families.

Noelle smiled warmly in several of the prints.

Oleo closed the wedding album and put it down in the green meadow full of wildflowers. Oleo snapped her fingers, and she disappeared . . .

≈

Bestselling author Dr. Audrey J. Levy is a story-teller at heart. It started when she was just 6 years old, spinning tales for her father by turning her weekly spelling words into a cohesive story while sitting in his lap. You are such a great writer, he told her. You're going to be very famous one day, he told her. Sounds idyllic, right? Well. Not so much.

In the years that followed, Audrey witnessed and experienced her father's old-fashioned method of discipline, which was a brief but certainly emphatic whipping with a red belt. His loud, frequent yelling was not music to her family's ears. As an adult, Audrey witnessed and experienced drug abuse, estrangement from her family, disinheritance by her parents, a 20-year union with a now-deceased alcoholic neuropsychologist, an attempted rape by an emotionally disturbed teenage male, and was told of three alleged family suicides, among other things. Pretty much the laundry list of dysfunctional family dynamics and co-dependency.

Despite all that, or perhaps because of all that, she likes to say, Audrey became a licensed Marriage and Family therapist and earned her Doctorate in Psychology. She also pioneered a journal writing method to help herself and others heal old wounds—finding hope, recovery, and redemption.

Audrey has written one novel, twelve screenplays, two novellas, two teleplays, and one stage play. She wrote, produced, and was the lead actress in her fifteen-minute short, "War and Family." Two of Audrey's screenplays made it to the finals of Mr. Steven Spielberg's Chesterfield Writing Competition, and a third screenplay made it to the finals of Mr. Redford's Sundance Competition. She currently lives on a houseboat in California with two four-legged kids.

≈

Look for *Adventure, Love, and Pirates*—
Book Three in
"The Adventures of Oleo" Trilogy